FALLBACK

B.G. Bradley

Praise for B.G. Bradley's Hunter Lake Series...

In Summer Rounds, Dale faces his biggest job ever—fixing his own broken marriage, family, and life. B. G. Bradley imbues this story of redemption with humor and humanity and surprise. He ambushes his readers with love, making Dale a character who restores faith in the goodness of people. Do yourself a favor. Take a trip to Hunter. Make some new friends. Don't be surprised if you never want to leave."

–Martin Achatz
Poet Laureate of the Upper Peninsula of Michigan

"I don't know why, but often before beginning a book I thumb through it, read the blurb, the back cover, see if chapters have titles, and glance at a few pages. I guess it's like kicking the tires of a car before you buy it. Admittedly, it's as pointless as judging a book by its cover, but this time after a quick look through Winter Heart *my first thought was this will never work. I was wrong, utterly wrong.*

"The poetry intermingled throughout the novel is essential to its success, the paragraphs and whole pages in italics with words here and there in bold type work, and the strange way in which chapters are sometimes separated into small, often only a paragraph in length, Parts 1, 2, 3, etc. does not interrupt the flow of the book. So I am publicly eating crow and praising the author for his creative approach to writing and formatting this very satisfying novel.

"This is the first in the author's Hunter Lake series. I'm eagerly looking forward to the next."

-Tom Powers, Michigan in Books Review
www.michiganinbooks.blogspot.com

*"*Winter Heart *is one of those hauntingly earnest books that stays with you long after you've read the final chapter. Every place has a spirit – that's what I believe – and B.G. Bradley perfectly captures the spirit of the book's setting, the "U.P.", the Upper Peninsula of Michigan. I've never been to the U.P.! But I know with certainty what like is like there now."*

-Arvid Nelson
Creator of the hit graphic novel series *Rex Mundi* and *Zero Killer*

"There's love in every sentence."

-Beverly Matherne
Poet and Author of *Bayou des Acadiens (Blind River)*

FALLBACK

a novel by
B.G. BRADLEY

Benegamah
Press

Hulbert Lake, MI
Canby, OR

Benegamah Press
Hulbert Lake, Michigan
Canby, Oregon

Cover photo by B.G. Bradley
Cover and book design by Matt Dryer

Printed in the United States of America

For the prodigal and his brother.

FOREWORD
By Martin Achatz

I have fallen in love with many places. When I honeymooned in Hawaii, I fell in love with coral beaches and pineapple stands, with Diamond Head looming volcanically over Waikiki, with warm thunderstorms that began every afternoon at 1:37 p.m. and ended 47 minutes later in dripping palm fronds.

When I was writing in Big Sur, I fell in love with freight train waves of the Pacific at 2 a.m., with otters hide-and-go-seeking in tide pools of kelp, with cormorants diving kamikaze into the ocean after flashes of silver fish, with the eel reek of sunning elephant seals, with the low crow of whales under the stars.

In New York City, I fell in love with caverns of skyscrapers, with swarms of theatergoers crowding subways at midnight, with Tuck (the guy at the deli who sold me an onion bagel dripping with cream cheese every morning), with the Algonquin where Dorothy Parker and Noel Coward drank themselves viciously drunk, with the ghosts of Ellis Island haunting the toes of Lady Liberty.

In Stratford, Ontario, I fell in love with a teenage girl who sat beside me in the Avon Theatre, weeping when Cleopatra's and Mark Anthony's bodies were carried offstage by soldiers. Fell in love with a pair of black swans gliding along the banks of the Avon River, with an elderly couple who sat on a bench, reading love sonnets to each other as dusk fell.

Yes, falling in love with new and exotic places is easy, because there is always the promise of home at the end of the romance. A return to the familiar, comfortable, and, ultimately, most sacred. It's why, at Thanksgiving, we gather with family and friends around a table to pray, laugh, and tell stories. It's why we watch old movies or re-read favorite books; *Casablanca* or *To Kill a Mockingbird*. All of these things hold fast and true in an impermanent world.

That's why I always love returning to Hunter, Michigan.

Hunter is a place I know. I know its streets and stores, trees and lakes. It's a place through which I could walk blindfolded from the local Catholic Church to my front door, avoiding all the broken sidewalks and knuckles of pine roots along the way. In the morning, I know the cars that go by on their way to work at the local newspaper or grocery store. In the summer, I hear kids screaming in the streets and can name each one and their parents. I could knock on any door in Hunter and be welcomed like a prodigal son. I'd be handed a cold beer, invited to a meatloaf dinner, regaled with town gossip, and given a warm bed to sleep in if I needed it.

That's what coming home is all about. It's finding a place where, no matter how long you've been gone or how far across the planet you've travelled, you will find family (through blood or love) who will kill that fatted-calf when they see you walking up the road. Whether you grew up in inner-city Detroit or on the tip of the Upper Peninsula of Michigan just a breath away from Canada, we all have Hunter in our DNA.

That is what B. G. Bradley reminds us in this book—in all his Hunter books. Home isn't just about geography or sociology or environment or climate. It isn't about a cabin by the lake or a mansion on a hill. It's something deeper, more profound. Flannery O'Connor once said, "The writer operates at a peculiar crossroads where time and place and eternity meet. His problem is to find that location."

B. G. Bradley has found that crossroads in Hunter, Michigan. Pack your bags. Rent a car. Book a flight. Set your GPS. Your destination is simple. One word. One syllable. An exhalation of breath.

Home.

–Martin Achatz
Poet Laureate of the Upper Peninsula

A wonderful fact to reflect upon, that every human creature is constituted to be that profound secret and mystery to every other.
−Charles Dickens

And it is clear that the soul must of necessity fall into many perils of falsehood, when it admits knowledge and reasoning; for oftentimes that which is true must appear false, and that which is certain doubtful; and contrariwise; for there is scarcely a single truth of which we can have complete knowledge.
−St. John of the Cross

Part I
In Bits and Pieces

Chapter I
Jake in the Car

Jesus, is that Ben?

Jake O'Brian watched from inside his government issue black sedan, parked on the side of the narrow and rough paved road that led up the hill from the village of Hunter southeast towards Hunter Lake. Behind the smoked glass windows he pondered the man coming towards him on an ancient bike.

It has to be Ben. That's the same nerd-friendly bike Grace bought him 25 years ago, complete with handle basket.

Okay, definitely Ben. The face still looks like him, but how much weight has he lost? Jen says almost seventy pounds. Never thought I'd say this, but he looks too skinny. Well, that's his business. And he's really tan. Good thing he never looks around at other people… He's so intense. So focused on whatever damned poem he's got going, or whatever else goes through that over analytical head. God I'd hate to be inside that skull. So much to worry about.

Uh oh, he's looking this way. Nah, he can't see in. But he's looking. Val must be having a good effect on him. He lives another twenty years, he might give up perseverating about everything and become a real boy.

He'd light me up if he knew what's going on with me.

Jen says he's changed. She seems frustrated about it. She's a bird. Always gotta know. Always worried somebody knows something she doesn't. Love that about her. Shiny.

Good thing I've done all the covert work over the years. They'll never even know I'm in town, unless I want them to. If Jen knew I was in town, and why, there'd be hell to pay from her too. So, I can't really talk to either one of my siblings about my situation, so what am I doing here? I've seen from a distance that they're both alive and well. Why wouldn't they be? Why am I here? What will being here help? To whom do I talk? Who do I tell about my wife and me? Now what?

Off goes my brother, onto the old railroad spur, now a "rails to trails" pathway. I had something to do with that, proud to say. He looks good. He really does. Guys get skinnier when they have a new love, until they get married, then they get fat. I haven't gained any weight though. Still shiny after all these years. But maybe that's just because I'm old and set in my ways. That's all it is really, just another way of being old. Nothing to be proud of, really. I just can't change. Set in my ways…really, that's it, if I'm honest with myself. Fuck honesty.

Of course, Christy can't cook at all. She never has really. Her parents kind of spoiled her. She's a spoiled, little…

How long am I going to sit here? I've seen him. What more is there? Do I need to stay in town? Who else do I need to see? What am I doing here? Maybe… Maybe I should see everybody. Everybody. Maybe I'll even track down Michael before I go back. If I go back. I don't know. I don't know.

I feel like a ghost. What the hell is happening here? Am I turning into Ben? Ben starts playing the ladies, well not really playing just going from monogamous to monogamous, but anyway he kind of takes my place and I take his? Is that it? I never wanted to be him. His life seemed so, I don't know, tight! Not shiny at all. He thinks about shit so much. I've always been for doing. Always! I mean, why did I get married? After all this time? I loved going from girl to girl. To be honest, two, three at a time. No questions, no commitments, just fun: shiny. There was always something new, always a new someone, a new game. A place, an accent, a person.

Women? Well, there are all kinds. And all kinds of ways to be when you're around them, to get around them. That's what

I used to think and everybody in the family gave me hell for it. I loved that. Shiny. Nice to be known for something. Nice to know people were saying, "You know that Jake!" "He's a player that Jake." "What a scamp that Jake is."

And now I'm married, just another old married guy. A cliche really. Married a trophy wife. Stuck, just stuck.

And now Ben is with Val. She's a travel agent for Christ's sake! How could the most fixed person in the world, my brother, end up with a fucking travel agent? What the hell? And she pokes at him, teases him, gets him up and moving and now he's lost 70 pounds! Seventy pounds at his age and that's, well, really hard. And once he decides to do something? Well, look the hell out. And he's really done it. He looks younger than I do.

Jen told me over the phone that Ben's mad as hell because everybody thinks he had chemo or an operation, though. So maybe I'm just imagining that he looks young because I'm feeling old. Jen said Ben was funny as hell spitting and sputtering about the chemo comments. I can just see him. But he's different now too, and not just physically. What's happening to him?

And Christy, well, she's great and likes to travel just like I do, but she's hinting not so subtly about a family and settling down somewhere, maybe outside Washington. Said maybe she'd teach, that I wasn't getting any younger. Do I really want little kids at my age? Hell, by the time they're 20, even if we had one this year I'll be 77, Well, that's not as old as it used to be. In Roman times 30 was good. In Shakespeare's 52 was very respectable. That's not the way now. And Dad, well he was dead at 54: three years younger than I am now.

Damnit! I am turning into Ben. Keep it shiny. Keep it shiny. I could do the grown up thing and go talk to my brother. I know what he'll say, though, and he'll be right. Grow the hell up! Make a decision and stick with it. Everything isn't meant to be shiny.

The hell with that. Who then? Mark? Jen? Ha, yeah if I want everybody in town to know I'm here. Stop over at the college talk to a few unfamiliar faces? How many are there? Somebody would see me sure. Would that be so bad? Make a decision Jakie boy! Go with the flow. Keep it shiny. But what if you don't like where this river is going?

Chapter 2:
Ben on the Bike

Holy shit! That was Jake! It had to be. Who else would have a government car and be in Hunter? He's going to make Donya really nervous if she sees that car. I better tip her off that it's just my idiot brother and not some other right-wing government idiot seeking to deport her. She's a great addition to that college. We can use all the diversity we can get and a brilliant, beautiful young professor from Afghanistan… Well, she's perfect for the needs of Hunter Woods College. She's just what all us whiter-than-white folks need in this town, especially those U.P. college kids. They always think they know the world. They don't really know their asses from a hole in the ground. Of course, neither did I.

Jake. What a goof! I remember the first time Kate told me she thought her Uncle Jake was a spy. I almost wet myself laughing. Oh, he's secretive enough, but he's…well…he's Jake. That kid, well he's what 57? Still a kid to me. Anyway, he couldn't be a spy if his life depended on it. He ever got caught by an enemy and they threatened torture, he'd tell them a joke. They'd laugh and let him go. That's just the way he is. Nobody would ever believe…

Ha, maybe he is a spy!

If he is, he should get better at stakeouts then. I mean, Jesus, if I could figure it out: the original absent-minded professor… Does he really think I don't know he's here? Does he forget our sister, Jen, and who and what she is? How much she talks? How much she tells everybody everything? Jake's wife, Christy, called her as soon as she got back from her trip, and told Jen her nutty husband, Jake, had disappeared saying something about a "secret mission" and signing it "love, shiny, Jake". What an asshole! Then she called my sweetheart Val and told her to watch out for government vehicles. Christy told Jen not to tell me and Val that they were having trouble or that Jake might be in town.

I love Val so, for so many reasons, but maybe most of all because she's a straight arrow. When Jen called and asked if she would keep a secret, Val told Jen that whatever she told her she was always going to tell me unless it would be hurtful. Jen sighed, Val said, and then told her everything anyway. My sister can't resist. Jen's got to have the scoop you know.

I guess I could have gone right up and tapped on the car window, but if he wants us to think he's hidden, I guess maybe he's got a good reason. It's probably commitment. That would be Jake's typical reason for giving a woman trouble: the woman wants a commitment and Jake's idea of a commitment is booking more than one night at a resort hotel. As far as I'm concerned fear of commitment is a pretty shitty reason to ditch somebody, especially somebody you claim to love, especially for Christ's sake, your wife. I guess he knows that's about what I would say about it too. So why is he spying on me? Maybe he wants me to bawl him out, tell him he's a bad boy, like I always have. Or maybe, probably more likely, he wants to see the vein stand out on my neck. He might be in for a surprise. I'm not really that guy anymore. I'm pretty happy.

I guess if he really wants to talk to me, the dumb shit will come and knock on the camp door. Whatever he does, it's his look out, not mine. Oh hell, he already knows what I think, why bother to talk to me? What's going on with him?

Twelve miles up the trail, over Porcupine Rise, cross the highway, and up the lake road. Val's waiting for me there, probably just woke up and the coffee is on at camp. I timed this out pretty well. I love coming home when she just wakes up. Just a small miracle to have that wonderful girl waiting for me early in the morning at the best place in the world. The dogs are waiting too.

Wonder if ol' Huck is feeling.good today. He's up and down. Mostly up, though. He beat that stroke and he still is getting around pretty well for the most part. I guess he'll go when he's damned good and ready. For that matter, so will I. Life is good.

Anyway, one half hour to Val! Life is good. "All will be well and all manner of things will be well."

Chapter 3
Jake's First Session with Mark

Transcript—Session 1 with Jake O'Brian.
Conducted by Mark O'Brian-Hicks, MS Psychology.

General comments: Jake has always been a hard nut to crack. This may be partially because I've known him most of my life and I'm personally involved. Where his older brother took his grief at the loss of his father and later his wife hard, and used the means of writing for the most part successfully to quell it, Jake seems untouched by…well…anything. This session was conducted, by his request at a nondescript government office building in Sault Ste. Marie, Ontario to which he somehow gained access. This for fear, he says, "That Jen (my wife, his sister) will find out I'm in the area and spread it around to anybody in earshot." I have news for him, but I'm under several oaths not to tell it.

(Transcript of recording, done by permission of Mr. O'Brian.)

Myself: Okay, well, why are we here?
Jake: Well, no big deal. Just trying to keep it shiny.
Myself:(   )
Jake: Okay, okay. If you're just gonna stare… Well, I sort of ditched Christy.
Myself: "Ditched"?

Jake: Well, I didn't drown her by the road side. I just sort of left her. Well…not exactly left…

Myself: What exactly then?

Jake: Well…I took off for a few days. It was all making me itchy.

Myself: (chuckle) Jake you are a Freudian's dream. "Itchy"? "took off"? And what's "it"?

Jake: (chuckles) Is that what you get paid for, to repeat people's choices of words back to them with a quizzical smile?

Myself: More or less. But coming from the family you come from, you have to know how important words can be.

Jake: (My note: an uncharacteristically sober tone) Of course.

Myself: (   )

Jake: Okay. Okay. Jeez. I'm feeling uneasy about being married, all right? And I swear if you repeat "uneasy" back to me I'm going to walk.

Myself: You wanted the session, Jake. Walk when you want.

Jake: Tough guy. (chuckles)

Myself: Takes one to know one. Why all the secrecy?

Jake: You mean generally, or just today?

Myself: Okay, both.

Jake: Shit. Me and my big…

Myself: Jake, what did you think this was going to be like?

Jake: This.

Myself: So if you didn't want to deal with whatever the issues are, why are we here?

Jake: (chuckles) Just trying to keep it shiny.

Myself: You know that expression is endearing to some people, but to people who really care about you…

Jake: Like you?

Myself: Of course. Jake, that word is infuriating. It reveals nothing, risks nothing, and gives you well…I hope you can take this…. power.

Jake: Shit.

Myself: Yeah. And your brother wants to punch you every time you use it.

Jake: Oh, that I know. That's why I use it as much as possible around him.

Myself: Why?

Jake: Get a rise out of him. Bust his balls.

Myself: That's pretty hostile…

Jake: Yeah, and immature too. I know. It's brothers.

Myself: Some brothers.

Jake: Me and my brother. Anything wrong with that?

Myself: Not here to judge.

Jake: Oh, bullshit! Of course you are. I hate that objective professional pose shit. I hate that!

Myself: Why?

Jake: Because it's false. It isn't the way things really are. I've worked negotiating legal contracts and documents in 15 countries now and people in every language always fall back on that, "I'm not judging" shit. Of course you're judging. It's human. It's what people do. Is it often a mistake to judge? Yes, but people still just naturally do it and it's the ultimate hypocrisy to pretend you don't.

Myself: Fair enough. Okay, I'm judging. I don't think that kind of shit, that needling each other all the time, mostly you him, frankly, is healthy even though I do it myself. The only thing that seems to bind you two sometimes is that rivalry, and that mutual attempt, mostly on your part, to aggravate the other.

Jake: Hey, don't judge. (chuckles) You don't think it works? The way Ben and I…okay, mostly me are…er is…whatever… (Little sigh) You don't think the relationship I have with my brother is healthy?

Myself: When was the last time you told Ben you love him?

Jake: He knows.

Myself: How do you know that?

Jake: Well, Jeez…I think he does.

Myself: When is the last time you told Christy you loved her?

Jake: Wow.

Myself: (   )

Jake: Well….I guess I don't do that enough for either of them. But I don't tell Jen or Mike I love them all the time and they seem to know.

Myself: Different cases. You of all people should understand that everybody needs to be handled the way they need to be handled. Everybody needs something different.

Jake: Well…yeah….that's true. I've seen that enough.

Myself: Why would it be any different with family then?

Jake: Shit. (Note: starts to cry a bit)

Myself: (   )

Jake: That might be enough for now.

Myself: You think?

Jake: Yeah.

Myself: You want to do this again?

Jake: I…dunno…yeah. I guess I better.

Myself: "better"?

Jake: Stop that shit. (chuckles)

Myself: Can't. It's the job.

Jake: Turn that off. And let's get out of here.

Myself: You're the boss, but I feel like I'm missing something.

Jake: (   ) You are. Christy told me something, by text of all things. The first part of it I already knew. It was hard not to notice really. The second part though… Said she wanted to tell me in person, but that I keep running away.

Myself: Do you think that's what you're doing?

Jake: Hard to deny. I live in Washington and I'm suddenly with you in Ontario.

Myself: Not ready to tell me what she told you?

Jake: Not yet. I need to take a trip first.

Myself: Okay. Maybe next time?

Jake: Maybe…if there is a next time.

Chapter 4
A New Girl in Town

Donya Abbasi-Sylvanus. Now there's a mouthful. Beautiful, girl…woman. I'd better watch that. Jake walked over to where Ms. Abbasi-Sylvanus was having coffee in the Hunter Lake College Library basement coffee shop. It was a little wood-paneled room. Mostly professors had coffee here. The kids hit the snack bar upstairs. Ms. Abbasi-Sylvanus was reading a copy of the New York Times and eating a scone. She was breathtaking, Jake thought. She wore conventional western dress, very well, he couldn't help noticing.

"Hello, Ms. Abbasi-Sylvanus. Everything shiny in your new job?"

Donya looked up from the Times and a smile immediately came to her face.

"Ah, Mr. O'Brian! I have so anticipated our meeting. Your sister said you might…show up…"

Holy shit! How did Jen…you dope…Donya is the prettiest, newest girl in town. Everybody in Hunter says so. I know everybody in Hunter. Christy told Jen to look for me of course, and Jen figured I'd head right for Donya. Some 'spy'…right…I've known spies and I'll never be one.

"I…"

She looked suddenly distressed. "Oh…oh…I'm so sorry. I didn't know that you meant to remain…ah…incognito…"

Jake laughed. "I guess…I guess where my sister and my

wife are concerned, there are no secrets."

"Well…"That look of distress was still there. "I am grateful to you and your family."

"Oh, Ms. Abbasi-Sylvanus…"

"Oh please, Donya, or Donni. That is much too long." Wide smile flashing dark eyes.

"Donni, then. The world is a very strange place."

She laughed and her laugh was enchanting. "Oh…indeed. You've heard the whole story then. Well, of course, you were going to help us with the…media."

"Have they finally forgotten you?"

"Thankfully yes. For now. Until the book comes out."

"Yes, I heard about that. I can't imagine a rough cuss like Dale writing a book, but I'm sure Jen as his ghost writer will steer him right.

"Oh, no doubt!" Big smile. "No doubt!" Donni had taken out a notebook with a leather cover and was writing something down.

"Notes for class?"

"After a fashion." She smiled a little embarrassed. "Actually I have just written down 'rough cuss'. I love American slang. It helps with my students."

"I'm afraid that one won't be much help. That's more of an idiom."

She did not look up from her writing. "Ah…like 'shiny'?"

Jake laughed very hard. This was one sharp lady. "How did you…?"

Now she looked up through her horn rimmed glasses and laughed, "Jen told me to watch out for a tall handsome man who used the word 'shiny' to punctuate his sentences."

Jake shook his head. "Well, I guess now she'll know I'm here."

"I'm afraid, as they say, that ship has already sailed."

"How long has my cover been blown?"

That smile. "Since you arrived in Sault Ste. Marie…'the Soo'… on Thursday."

"How did…"

"Apparently a hotel clerk there is in a book club with your sister."

"Small world."

"Yes, this is something I am learning, but I like it. Now," her look became more focussed. "How may I help Mr. Jacob O'Brian?"

"Jake."

"Jake."

"Oh, just passing the time, really. Cooling my heels for a while in the home town. It's all shiny. And I wanted to meet you. The story is so strange…so odd that you would wind up here of all places."

"Perhaps. Then again, perhaps nothing happens by accident. And I'm told that nothing you do…pardon me for being ah, blunt, is ever, shall we say, uncalculated."

"Ouch."

She looked back down at her notes. "I hope I did not offend." She smiled.

"Oh…no…you are smart to let me know the lay of the land. I do have a tendency to…well…gawk at beautiful women."

A very sober look came up to greet Jake. "So I am told, and thank you for the compliment." It was punctuated by an engaging smile. "Certainly no offense. Have you spent any time in Afghanistan? I believe the law is your concern?"

"Just a little. I helped for a few weeks with the new constitution. And I've been there several other times since, but I was only a boots-on-the ground guy for a week or two. I worked, for the most part, by the internet from Washington on that project."

She said a few words in a language Jake did not understand. At a gathering just over a year later, she would translate them to him as, "You saw my country 'through a glass darkly' then."

"Excuse me?"

"Ah…no Farsi then?"

"Very little. French, German, Russian, Italian, Spanish, Mandarin, Vietnamese, even Irish Gaelic, just to trace my heritage, but when I was learning languages for my work, nobody saw the

Mideast coming. Anyway..that's what Christy does."

"Christy is your wife, yes?"

"Yes…and my translator. That's how we met."

"Oh, yes, but I had heard you met through your nephew, ah, Michael."

Jake blushed. "Well, yes, so the story goes."

Donya smiled a teasing smile, "Is it a true story?"

"Well…yes, I'm afraid so." He laughed and said idly, "Everybody knows that story now, I guess."

"I'm afraid so. Yes. But I hope I am not being rude."

"No, I think you're just being you. And you've got your guard up. I don't blame you."

Donni laughed for a long moment. "I understand the talk of your charms now Mr. O'Brian."

"Jake."

That smile again, "No, I believe it had better be Mr. O'Brian until you find your way back to Christy." She looked around the coffee shop in a theatrical way. "This is a very small town after all and my husband, even with a still somewhat lamed leg, is a very large and Irish man. With a temper to match. And his father well…"

Jake laughed loud and long, until all eyes had focused on him. Then he nodded three or four times before putting out his hand and shaking Donya's.

"Charmed I'm sure. And touche. Send my regards to Jen."

"Hadn't you better do so yourself, Mr. O'Brian?"

"Yes, I guess so. As soon as possible."

He gave a nervous little informal wave and left the coffee shop.

Several of her colleagues gave Donya knowing looks.

"So," she said. "I've met 'the player'."

The room erupted in laughter and Donya sipped her coffee.

Chapter 5
Jen's Kitchen

"Did you really think I wasn't going to know you were here? Did you really think I wouldn't tell everybody to look out for you. You know, Jake, I've been looking out for you forever. I don't want anybody to punch you."

"I can handle myself."

"Even with a broken leg," she said laughing, "Ike could put you in the hospital. You're middle-aged and you were never that tough to begin with."

"Hey."

"I'm too old for bullshit. Now, I'm glad you're seeing Mark. The big jerk didn't even tell me…I'm glad you did."

"I"m starting to wish I hadn't. And Mark does have that obligation of confidentiality…"

"Yeah, there's that."

"Seriously, I think it's helping."

"Enough to go back to your wife?"

"One step at a time."

"Jake O'Brian you've broken that girl's heart! Do you know that?"

"I…"

"You get your ass back to see her. And you stay away from Donni Abassi-Sylvanus. She's a sweet innocent…"

"Some 'sweet and innocent'. That woman cut me to pieces

in five seconds."

"Really? Jake, were you hitting on her? I knew you'd find her when you got to town. Does marriage mean anything to you? You and the pretty girls!"

"I was not hitting on her. I…just wanted to see what the fuss was about. She is…well…quite lovely. I saw her at the coffee shop, an hour ago. I guess your sources are slipping. So…Ben knows too?"

"Of course. It takes a village…"

Jake's face reddened, partly in embarrassment, partly in stifled anger, "To spy on an idiot?"

"Ha! A note of humility! What's this?"

"Middle age…" Jake shook his head.

"Oh for heaven's sakes…" Jen's eyes widened. Was Jake changing?

"Late middle age actually. Jen…what am I doing?"

"Leaving Christy? That's exactly what…"

"With Christy," Jake dropped his eyes, looking at his expensive Italian shoes.

Jen looked hard at Jake. "That's something I guess you should have thought of before."

"But I didn't."

"But you didn't."

"So there it is." Jake looked up sadly at Jen. There was a long, long silence in which the old family clock in the front hall chimed the hour.

"I guess, I'll be on my way."

"Home?"

"I dunno to be honest."

"There's no hiding place here, Jake."

"I know."

"Go home."

"I might."

"What else might you do?"

"I really don't know."

"Well, sit right there and have some eggs."

"I…"

She shot him a look.

"Fine. Women in this town are in league against me."

"Women everywhere are in league against you. The ones who haven't lost their senses to your boyish charms, at least."

"Yikes." Jake forced a laugh.

"Exactly."

Jen began fixing the eggs and in the process texted Christy with the latest.

Jake noticed.

"Expanding the gossip mill?"

"Texting your wife."

"Oh…shit…" Jake started to stand.

"Just to let her know you're here and okay."

"Couldn't you have waited until I left?" His face reddened again.

"She needs to know."

Jake sighed. "Okay. Tell her I love her."

"Why don't you?"

"She knows."

Jen looked hard at Jake. "You sure?"

"Jesus, why is everybody asking me that?"

"Why do you think?"

Jake nodded once, then said, "You know Mom used to say that if you tell people you love them all the time, they may come to think you're 'protesting too much' and come to believe you don't really love them."

"Mom wasn't right about everything." Jen looked hard and long at Jake with an expression that was direct from their mother's repertoire.

"You wouldn't say that if she was still alive," Jake said, his old smirk back for a fraction of a second.

"You wouldn't have left Christy if she was still alive," the borrowed expression never wavered.

"Touche'. Okay, then. Shiny. All shiny."

Jen looked down at a returning text from Christy. "Thank

God!" It said.

Jen looked up, "Why don't you call…"

Jake was gone.

"That boy…" she said.

Chapter 6
Meeting Michael in the Mountains

The hike had been way too long: a solid five hours at least. The mountain air and elevation, the crazy pace at which Michael pushed the so called "little walk": all that was wearing on his mind, and, yes, so was late middle age and the puzzle that was his current situation with Christy.

Ahead, at last, was the summit. It really hadn't looked that bad when they started uphill from the Daybreak Summit workers' apartments where Michael was currently couch surfing. And Michael's "little walk" comment had comforted him. A little walk might clear his head, make him able to pick just the right words, not fluster the poor kid, who probably was almost as much of a victim, what with his syndrome, as Jake was, in this whole Christy thing.

"Just a little walk, Unc. It'll clear your head. You worry too much," Michael had said, when he'd arrived five hours ago. Yes, that had been comforting, but being told he worried too much…well, that was new.

Now, here they were, high in the Canadian Rockies, on a crisp Fall day. Up above the tree line, the sky crystalline blue. This is where he would die, no doubt. At least his body was telling him so. Why not? It was a beautiful day for it.

Jesus, I'm thinking like Ben, or like Ben used to. What the hell is happening? In truth, Christy and Michael would be better matched together than he and Christy were anyway. He thought back to the day he met Christy. Back when he was still a player. The family was scandalized when it finally came out that Christy and Michael had once been an item. The assumption was that Jake had stolen her, but that wasn't exactly true. Michael had asked Christy if she… well…fancied his uncle, she'd said yes, and Michael'd immediately given the whole thing his blessing. He confided later to Jake that he was kind of relieved. It might be the best thing in the world if he died here, and gave Christy back to Michael. Serve Michael right for slipping him a poison pill to begin with. The player really got played and by a kid who didn't even know he was playing. Or did he? Had Michael planned it this way? No, of that he was certain, Michael never planned anything.

Michael pulled off his ancient Tiger's ball cap, the one from 1984 that Ben had given him, ran his hand over his short blond hair, before replacing it, took a pull from the hose of his water pack, and took out a power bar, offered Jake one, which he deferred by saying, between gasps, "No thanks. Those things taste like shit. Always have."

Michael was already on to something else. Jake looked where he was gazing out over a rocky outcropping. An eagle was circling.

"If that was a vulture, I'd swear he was coming for me," Jake said.

Michael looked over, his face as usual, a bemused puzzle. It was so hard to read the kid. "Why so glum, Unc?"

"Never mind. Let me catch my breath."

Michael looked back at the eagle, "It was just a little walk. Didn't used to wear you out so much."

"Thanks for mentioning that. I was getting too full of myself."

"You're welcome."

"I…"

Michael looked over, truly puzzled.

"Never mind." Jake wiped away a huge dollop of forehead sweat. "Look, I wanted to talk to you."

Michael looked over blank again.

"There's something important I need to say."

Still, disconcertingly blank.

"It's…it's…Christy."

"Heard you left her. Wondered when that would happen."

"You did?" Now he felt completely at a loss.

"Well, sure, Unc. Your track record speaks for itself." He looked back at the eagle. "Wonder what he's thinking."

"Jesus…How can you be so…" He stopped. No matter how many times you had a conversation with Michael, it was impossible not to be taken aback at his matter-of-fact and uniform way of dealing with every subject, grave or mundane. It might be a syndrome, Aspergers as diagnosed, or it might just be as Grace and Ben had always claimed, "Michael being Michael". Whatever it was, it sure was taking Jake out of his game right now. Michael was shooting him that blank look again. "Never mind," he said a third time, realizing that he might just as well get to it. "Christy is pregnant…and she says it isn't mine."

Michael's expression didn't change. He looked back at the eagle, "Huh. Whose is it?"

Jake counted ten trying not to fly off the handle in exasperation. It would do no good at all and only confuse Michael. He decided to try the matter-of-fact approach, since everything with Michael was a mater of fact. "She's six months along and I was thinking about that day we met you, on our honeymoon. You know when we met at the Great Wall?"

Michael's face finally took on an expression: pleasure. "That was fun. Thanks for paying my way there."

"That's not the point, Mike."

"Michael. My name's 'Michael'." Finally a note of emotion which faded instantly.

Jake came very close to losing it. Again he composed himself, while Michael looked on again implacable. "Remember that first night?"

"Yeah, you were tired. You went back to the hotel, so Christy and I went out, saw the sights."

"Yes, exactly. Anything happen that night? Maybe you two got a little drunk and something happened, for old time's sake. Old lovers…you know…"

"We had tea."

"You…"

"Had tea and Christy talked about how much she loved you. How well everything was going." He looked back up at the eagle. "Must be something to eat up there. They don't just fly for fun. What would be up there?"

"Michael…"

"Yeah?" He finally looked back, his expression still blank.

"Now…now I won't be mad. Shit happens, but was there anything other than tea?"

"I think I had a scone, maybe a sandwich. Yes, cucumber I think…"

"Michael did the two of you…you know…get together for old time's sake…"

"Well, yeah. That was the whole point right?"

"It was?"

"Well, sure. That's what you said when you invited me, that Christy and I could talk things over for old time's sake…"

"No…no…I mean did you, and again, if you did, you did, it's just water over the dam. I won't be mad. Did you get physical?"

"No. It was dark by then and Christy never likes hiking at night…"

"Jesus Christ…did the two of you, you know…get intimate?"

Michael shot a look of puzzlement at Jake which suddenly turned into an absolutely beatific smile, "You mean, did we fuck?"

"Um…yes…" Jake let out a long exasperated gasp.

"Well, no. You two are married, right?" He looked back up at the eagle.

Jake's knees were suddenly wobbling. It was bad enough so that Michael actually noticed.

"Unc, you don't look good. You should probably sit down."
Jake did, rather suddenly. The rock beneath him felt good.
Solid. Many had sat here before and the top was smoothed out. He
wondered if anybody had ever sat here before with thoughts similar
to the ones now in his head.

He looked up at the eagle that Michael was watching again.
Jake had flown across the continent to have a kind of showdown
with his nephew, intending to give him, syndrome or no, a piece
of his mind, or at least find out what he knew, and he'd instead
been confronted by the totally innocent, implacable enigma which
was Michael Jacob O'Brian. He held tight to the rock outcropping
hoping for stability. At last he spoke.

"What the hell is going on?"

"That's what I wonder, Unc. I'm definitely putting this in
my next blog. Maybe somebody else will have an idea."

"No! You can't put this in your blog."

Michael looked thoroughly confused. "Why not?"

Jake hardly knew what to say. He began to laugh. He
stopped, got serious. "Michael, it would be a violation of trust. Of
family."

"What family? The eagle's?"

Now it was Jake's turn. "What? Oh...oh...Are talking
about the goddamned bird?"

"Well, yeah. I was wondering what food source is up there."

"Jesus, I thought you were talking about...":

"What?"

"Never mind..."

"Oh. Ha! Oh. I get it. You thought I was talking about
Christy and you and me...No, I'd never put that in the blog. That
would be, well, just mean." He looked back towards the eagle,
then said, "Really, I can't believe you're surprised she slept with
somebody else."

Jake didn't know whether to punch his nephew or just
marvel at his inability...unwillingness? to think like anybody else.
He decided to marvel and learn more. "Why...why not?"

"Well, c'mon. Look how quick she jumped from me to

you. She's always been like that. Thought you knew. You of all people." He looked back up at the rock.

"Yeah." He took a long breathe. There was nothing to say. "Let's head down. I'll take you to lunch."

"Oh good." Michael said, already oblivious again. "I'm outta cash."

Chapter 7
Jake on the Plane
With an Exhausted Irishman

He'd gotten drunk because he frankly didn't know what else to do. He'd had at least three little bottles of whisky and perhaps one of gin, maybe two, the first three mixed with Seven Up, the next in a martini and now, back to Seven and 7, he was ignoring the 7-Up can completely and drinking right from the tiny bottle.

Okay, so it's definitely not Michael. But if not, Mike, who? Whom?

"I've never seen the aurora before," said the exhausted Irishman in the seat next to him. Liam was his name, Jake thought he remembered, or Ian or maybe Sean....no that was Jake's nephew... what was this guy's name? He was usually very good with names. Oh, fuck it.

"Huh? I mean, pardon me?"

"The aurora. Look!"

Jake looked out the window and even in his state of inebriation, it was amazing. There on the horizon, which clearly curved at this height, was the massive and colorful wall of the aurora borealis.

He couldn't really remember what he'd said to Liam or Ian, or Patrick? Maybe it was John. Just John. Fuck it! He believed he'd told him the whole Christy scenario and the Irishman...

Liam, definitely Liam…had told him his whole story about the call coming from Calgary where his favorite aunt, her name was Mary, Jake thought he remembered, or Patsy or…fuck it! had suddenly died after a long and wonderful 97 year life. 97. Funny that he remembered that, in his current state, so clearly. Liam, definitely Liam, or Joshua…Fuck it! was staring at him.

Finally Jake said, "Cool." *That's a funny word. It has to do with temperature. Why does temperature have anything to do with it? With what? What was it we were discussing? Anyway, we discussed it until we found it disgusting…*

Jake laughed out loud and maybe Liam shot him a quizzical look.

"Cool, yes. Indeed. Indeed. Puts a cap on a real trip, quite a trip for me. I'm exhausted, but I'll sort it all out later."

It took a moment for Jake to sort out the Irishman's meaning. At last, Jake managed, "Yup…yup…me too. Don't know what coulda…coulda done…er…gone better."

Liam looked him over again, assessing. Then the Irishman smiled. Jake wondered if he knew how drunk Jake was. He decided he did. Why not? Everybody else knew everything about him. Even good ol' innocent-as-the-day-he-was-born Asparagus… er, Aspergers Michael. Oh…that wasn't fair…that kid was just… Michael. He couldn't help being who he was. Good kid. And he'd given him Christy. Kind of just deeded her over. And Christy had gone along with it. He hadn't really thought it was weird at the time. And Christy had looked so good that day in Tibet, when, on a lark he'd met the two of them. They were on the verge of getting married, sort of on their honeymoon…er…pre-marriage honeymoon. Lots of honey and mooning anyway! He laughed out loud and the Irishman perhaps named Liam smiled and chuckled a bit, then rolled over to sleep.

Yup, Michael and Christy had been all but married then. At least, Christy seemed to think so. That's what she'd said. That was how she'd put it when things, that very day, started to happen between them. She was a beauty. A real spitfire. And full of substance. Not like most girls, women…he'd better watch that…he'd dated.

She had substance. She was solid. Just like her parents. Wasn't she? Should he be grateful or spiteful towards Mike about that deeding her over thing? Anyway…anyway. He was just Michael, Ben's honest son, his honest nephew, that was certain. He didn't do anything dishonest or out of malice. That he could take to the bank. Which bank he wondered. The bank of marriage? The bank of love? The bank of trust in family. "In family we trust". What would the money look like from that bank? Would it have Ben's picture on it or Jen's? Or would it have both of them on it arguing with each other? He was really drunk.

The question came back into his dizzy head again. *If not Michael, then who? Whom?* Why hadn't he just put the question to her: "Who did you sleep with, Christy?"

It was just five little words. No six. Was it six? Anyway, who? Whom? Oh, fuck it. Who fucked her? Why hadn't he just said, "Who fucked you?"

She was crying. That's why. That was always why. She'd start to cry and then he was lost. He'd always been lost when women cried. That was the pattern. They'd cry: he'd take off. Fuck crying. He didn't like it. It was that simple. He didn't like when women cried. Who did? Why not leave? It was unpleasant, so you left. Very logical. He didn't like it when anyone cried really. Not ever. Not at least since Dad died all those years ago. Too many tears in that house. Too many tears. Why not leave? Life was about being happy. Happiness begins at home. Keep it shiny.

No tears in my house. Not now, not ever. If the tears start, you find a new home, or you go back to your own home, like I did after Ben's Grace died. He was pretty sure Kate, Ben's other kid, still hated him for that. But Jen didn't. Good ol' Jen. What was the Frost line that Ben was always quoting? Oh, yeah…oh yeah…'No more to build on there'. Death ain't a rock, like that nice rock up in the mountains in Banff…funny name, "Banff". Sounds like the person saying it is drunk. The person saying it is drunk… Anyway, anyway, Christy was crying and that was it. She couldn't talk and all he was gonna hear from her even if she did was something unpleasant. Another way he'd failed her. Fuck that.

"So, so why not leave?"

Possibly Liam looked up at him through sleepy eyes. "Excuse me?"

"Oh…oh…nothing L–Liam… Just thinking out loud."

"Ah…the name is Seamus. Yes. Well, the thinking aloud happens at our age, lad. No cause for concern." He smiled. "Much as I'd like to keep looking at the aurora, I'd better get some sleep. I have many miles to cover back to Dublin."

"You…you do that."

There was another line…Frost too…'And miles to go before I sleep.' That was where he was right now. Miles to go down this fucking rabbit hole Christy had made for him. Course, he had something to do with it too. Takes two to tango, or maybe three. Definitely takes at least two to fuck, but which two? Christy was one, but who, whom, fuck it, was the other? He was drunk and wide awake and he had something to find out. But from who? Whom? Fuck grammar. But where to go? Where now?

"Who did Christy fuck?"

"Hmm…" said certainly Seamus before falling back asleep.

He suddenly had a picture of her face in tears. Christy crying. Trying to tell him who it was. And he couldn't deny it. He couldn't deny it. He was very careful that the next thought didn't come out aloud and wake undoubtedly Seamus…that was it… wasn't it? yet again.

I love her so much.

And then he started to cry.

"Damnit!"

"Hmmgh…" said almost positively Seamus. And back to sleep.

"I envy you, pal, Liam ol' buddy," Jake said wiping away tears and taking another long pull from the tiny Seven Crown emptying it completely.

"Stewardess?"

Chapter 8
Jake's Second Session
with Mark

Transcript—Session 2 with Jake O'Brian. Conducted by Mark O'Brian-Hicks, MS Psychology.

General comments: Jake is showing signs of grief and compassion for the first time in his life, I think. At least the first time I've ever seen it from him.

Myself: Okay. So, what now? What the hell should I do?
Jake: You tell me.
Myself: Not my job.
Jake: What is your job?
Myself: Listening.
Jake: Fuck you.
Myself: (laughing) That's a little hostile. Do you mind if I ask you a question?
Jake: It would be a refreshing fucking change.
Myself: Why did you leave?
Jake: There it is.
Myself: ( )
Jake: Okay. Okay. Christy's pregnant.
Myself: Oh…well congrats…

Jake: No, you don't get it…

Myself: Oh…I think I do…

Jake: Shoot.

Myself: The whole commitment thing?

Jake: Why does everybody think that? 'Jake's afraid of commitment, so he just takes off whenever there's danger of one.' Why do they all believe that?

Myself: Why do they?

Jake: Oh…fuck you Mark! The kid isn't mine.

Myself: Oh…oh…shit…oh okay. Didn't see that coming.

Jake: Neither did I.

Myself: Oh…oh… No! You just went to see Michael. Is it his?

Jake: That's what I thought, and that's why I went, but no.

Myself: You sure?

Jake: I asked him point blank and he said no. And you know that kid is incapable of lying.

Myself: Yes…yes he is. Well, shit.

Jake: Yeah, I know, 'Who then?'

Myself: Or 'whom'. Wow. You've surprised me today, Jake, I gotta admit.

Jake: I'm surprising myself.

Myself: Why?

Jake: I still love her.

Myself: (   )It's okay. Here. Use my hanky. Do you want to quit for now?

Jake: No. No let's keep this going. For once I'm going to have to cry. I'm going to have to watch somebody cry.

Myself: Christy?

Jake: Yeah, I hung up when she started crying trying to tell me who the father was. And now I feel like shit about it. I need to go back, deal with the tears, hers and mine, and hear her out…or something.

Myself: Well…

Jake: Well what?

Myself: Well, that's progress.

Jake: It is? Well then progress feels like shit.

Myself: Yup. In matters of the heart, it usually does. You know…

Christy is at our house.

Jake: She is?

Myself: Yeah.

Jake: I should go talk to her, huh? And don't say, 'What do you think?'

Myself: Yeah, I think you should. Work it out, one way or the other. At least find out who the father is?

Jake: Is that important?

Myself: Oh…oh…maybe not… I'm impressed, Jake. Even thinking that is…

Jake: Progress?

Myself: Well, it's probably the most adult thought you've ever had.

Jake: Fuck you. (laughs.)

Myself: (Laughs.)

Chapter 9
Christy and Jake
in Jen's Kitchen

Of course somewhere Jen was listening in, probably watching too: through a key hole, through a slot in her bedroom floor, hell she probably had bugs she'd bought from covert sources. She was much more of a spy than he would ever be. It didn't matter. Whatever came out of this conversation would be all over Hunter in under an hour anyway. It didn't matter how it got there. Jake sipped his coffee.

Should I tell Christy Jen is listening? No. The hell with her! She's lying to me right now.

Even knowing that, Jake still loved her. But there was no doubt. Flashing those pretty blue eyes, tossing that glossy dark bobbed hair, twisting her gorgeous mouth, pouting lips into pained contortions, she was lying to him. There was not a single doubt in his mind that what she was saying was an absolute lie.

Dammit! It doesn't make any difference! I still love her! I even love that she's lying. I even love the mystery of why she is lying. It's intimate. It's just for me and I'm the only one who knows for certain she is lying.

She had just told him that the baby was Michael's. Now she was crying. He leaned over, set down his coffee and hugged her.

"Oh, oh, I don't deserve you. How…how…can you be so kind? I thought you'd be so angry!"

"We'll work it out. What's the point of being angry? It is what it is. I've been a shit all my life and it's come back to me."

"No…no, not to me. Never to me. You've been such… such a prince to me! And I've done this terrible thing with Michael. How can you forgive me?"

She was lying. Michael was telling the truth. Just the way he'd said, "Well no. You two are married, right?" Like a little boy stating a basic moral lesson he had learned, from two of the most moral people who'd ever lived: Ben and Grace. Anyway, Michael doesn't lie. Can't lie really. Ben and Grace used to laugh at his attempts to lie. The boy isn't capable of subterfuge. He is even less a spy than I am. Did it matter that she was lying to him? No. It was flattering really. Whoever's child this was, he would raise it without a moment's hesitation. He loved her. Should he just say that to her?

It came out before he had time to think it over. Like the words of the Oracle at Delphi.

"You don't have to lie, baby. We'll raise the baby together no matter…"

Christy looked up, stunned, and for a second absolutely caught. Now he was sure.

"I'm….I'm not lying."

"It's okay. I don't care. The child is ours."

Her lower lip began to quiver. "You…you don't believe me?"

"I did…or rather I thought it must be Michael's myself, so I went and talked to him."

"You…"

"I asked him straight out and he said, and I quote…" He couldn't help smiling at the memory and Christy stared at him with an expression of wonder. "'No, you two are married, right?'"

Christy started to laugh. Then she laughed harder. She stopped suddenly, "That's so, Michael. But, but, you think I'm lying."

"It doesn't matter…"

Why didn't I keep my mouth shut?

At that moment his cell phone buzzed in his pocket. He

ignored it. It kept buzzing.

"Oh…oh…answer it. I need time to…to think about this…you're being sweet in a way, but you think I'm lying…Oh… what's the use of pretending. I am lying." She sobbed for a moment, then looked up at the next buzz of the phone. "Oh, answer the damned phone!"

It was a text from his partner in O'Brian and Maki, the government-affiliated firm he'd started all those years ago, to aid in international relations. Jerry "Bump" Maki, was the son of Jim "Bash" Maki, the hard-nosed little pug who'd been his arch rival in basketball all those years ago. Point guard for the Soo. He'd have to catch up with his old pal Bash one of these days. Bash was a banker in the Soo. He'd opened his own bank with a couple of other locals. He'd taken on Bash's lawyer son, shown him the ropes and one thing had led to another. Now they were partners and his plan had been for Bump to take over the firm.

But what if the baby becomes a lawyer?

He looked at the text, "Dude! Where are you? Shit hitting the fan here. When you coming back?", it said.

He thought it over. Maybe the best thing would be just to go back to Washington with Christy as soon as possible. They could talk on the plane out of Jen's earshot.

"Directly," he texted back. And returned the phone back to his pocket.

"Let's go, honey."

"Where?"

"Home."

"Really? You…you don't care who the baby belongs to?"

"He or she belongs to us."

She started to cry again. "If you want to know. If you really want to know. I'll tell you."

"It…it doesn't matter unless it matters to you."

She cried again. "Okay. Okay. I'll think. I'll think that over. You're sure?"

"Well…no…but I'm saying so." He shot her a waggish half grin.

She playfully slapped his cheek lightly. Then leaned in and kissed him hard.

"You're...you're so evolved."

Jake laughed. "Nobody has ever accused me of that before. I wish Ben could hear you."

She flinched for a second. "Ben?"

"Yeah, he'd get a big kick out of somebody thinking I was evolved. He thinks I'm the worst player going. He's always telling me I can't be Peter Pan forever."

"Oh. Oh sure." She said.

Chapter 10
Jake in His
Washington Office

What the hell?

The thought kept recurring to him, nagging at him. And the supposed shit storm here was nothing. A little language barrier that Bump and Christy (mostly Christy) cleared up over the phone on a conference call in fifteen minutes. They worked well together, Christy and Bump. In fact, working with Christy was the only way Bump worked well. He wasn't his dad. He wasn't Bash. He wasn't as smart. He wasn't as folksy. He wasn't as calculating. He wasn't as sharp in any way as his banker father. He wondered why he'd taken Bump on at all. Sometimes the kid couldn't find his ass with both hands. How could he ever take over the firm? But after all this time, if he didn't give the kid the firm, his old man would never forgive Jake. He valued old friends. He'd pissed off most of them over the years by sleeping with their wives or girlfriends. He'd never slept with Bash's wife, Betty, which was interesting because Betty was a Hunter girl. A Hunter girl and cheerleader who only had eyes for the point guard from the Soo: Bash. She was one of the few girls in Hunter who wouldn't give Jake the time of day. He'd tried with her while they were still in high school and after that. Even once at a reunion after she and Bash had been married. She'd slapped his face, and told him if he ever tried again she'd tell Bash. He wasn't afraid of Bash, well maybe a little, but the real reason he'd never tried again was that he wanted to keep Bash as a friend. Why? It was simple really: Bash had won a girl Jake couldn't. This impressed Jake. Maybe that's why they'd become and remained friends.

He shifted a few papers into a manilla file, stuck them in his desk. All done here for now. Bump was handling the rest of the cases with the junior partners. The whole idea had been for he and Christy to have a kind of semi-honeymoon for a year, to test out Bump's abilities. But if he was going to think there was a shit storm every time things got a little well…bumpy…what was the point? Oh well…once he passed the firm on, it wouldn't be his worry. And he was tired of worrying. He just wanted to be with Christy and be in love and have all the things…

Ben…

There it was again. He looked out the window towards the British embassy across the street. He had a lunch with Nigel Chalmers, so very British, planned for that day. No business, just lunch, long lunch and drinks. He and Nigel, two old dogs finally settled down. Nigel had had a young wife too, and he'd left her. In fact he'd told Jake not to marry Christy. Hadn't come to the wedding for that very reason. But he'd called the other day, before all the baby stuff, and it had sounded good. Lunch with Nigel was something Jake had absolutely loved when he was still single. It had made him feel so cosmopolitan, so sophisticated, but now there was Christy and in all honesty he had no wish for babes with the drinks. He felt no need for covert ops with the opposite sex any more. He had Christy. The real question was: 'Who had Christy had?' ' Rather whom'? In this case, correct grammar might be appropriate.

She flinched when I mentioned Ben.

Oh for Christ's sake. There is no way. I mean, Ben? He loved Grace so much! Almost killed him. And now he's got it for Val just as bad. There is no way. He is the least likely candidate of all.

Jake laughed out loud at the thought, but the laughter was uneasy.

Why else would she flinch, though, when I mentioned him? She's…she's just worried he'll find out. Maybe through Jen. And then, what would he think of her? That's it. That's it.

He had had this thought before. He'd run this whole sequence on the plane two dozen times at least. Somehow it hadn't convinced him.

Come on, that's insane! When would it even have happened? I was with him the night before the reception! And the night of the reception there was only that one time when they were alone…

He'd run this thought before too, three dozen times. She'd been drunk, and she'd walked over and kissed Ben on the cheek, and Ben had been embarrassed and flattered and they'd danced then, which Ben never did and then she'd led him off into an adjoining room off the lobby. And beyond that room was a stairway to upstairs at the hotel. And they'd been gone for over an hour.

Oh for Christ's sake! My brother would not do that! Not ever, but certainly not at the reception. And Christy…Christy wouldn't…well, she did it with someone. Unless…unless…she's lying about that, testing me… I did piss Ben off by making fun of his drowning story, and he'd had a lot to drink too, but it takes a lot for him, tough old cuss.

"Not shiny. Not shiny at all."

No, no, this was ridiculous. Ben was already raving about Val by then. He's strictly monogamous. She was even there that night… But he didn't know that. As far as he knew he was unattached. And he's always had this passive aggressive thing about me. What better way to stick it to me than by…sticking it to Christy? Oh that's pretty crass. Can't blame him, really, if it's true. I've mostly been a shit to him. To everybody really. If it's true, if it's Ben's, I've got it coming. I've really got it coming. Well, if it is Ben's, it will probably look just like him, and if so, just like me. So nobody but Christy and me will ever know. Except Jen, of course. She'll find out. And then everybody will know. Fuck it. It doesn't matter. I don't care. The baby will be ours, mine and Christy's.

Maybe…maybe the baby is mine. Maybe Christy is just testing me. Seeing how I'll react, if I'll stick by her. What kind of a person does that? A crazy one. Jesus, I should talk. Maybe it's all the stories she's heard. Maybe that walk with Ben was when she heard all the stories from him about all the girls I've been with. No… Ben wouldn't have poisoned the well. The worst he would have done…well…Ben might have said, 'You sure about this marriage thing? You know what he's like, right?' kind of playfully. She would have smiled at him. And he'd have said, 'Okay. My job is done.' Maybe…maybe she found that charming though. Maybe really charming. Who knows? Maybe that's what led to…

"Oh, come on. Come on. You're losing it."

She did it with somebody else, though. That's certain… Maybe… Unless the testing me thing is true… Who else? Was it Ben? All I know is, it wasn't Michael. Unless…unless… he's learned how to lie. I know he's had a few sessions with Mark to help him deal with people socially. He's given him some pointers. Maybe inadvertently Mark made Mike realize how he could manipulate people… What if it is Michael's? What if I've thought my way out of the truth and Christy couldn't be happier? Is Christy the enemy? I love her so much, but I'm thinking such bad things about her. Jesus Christ… I'm going to go out of my mind here. Lunch. Lunch with Nigel. Maybe that will…I'm canceling lunch…Got to see Christy….but…but if I do, I'll just upset her. I don't want to upset her.

"Jesus, Jake, get a hold of yourself."

He looked down at the file. He opened the desk and reached in for the file again. He half-heartedly looked it over. Afghanistan. He'd been there a number of times… And always found a way to get the hell out of there as quickly as possible. Tough place. Tough people. Donya Abassi…

That Donni was something, huh? She would be something naked. What the fuck? Ike would kick my ass! Christy would disown me.

You're flattering yourself, O'Brian. Donya already kicked your ass. And she wasn't even trying. How in the hell can I think like this? It's the old me. It's just easier to be a shit. For once…for once I'm not gonna be a shit.

"Shit."

He took out his phone and found Mark's number on his contacts.

Chapter II
Jake's Third Session
With Mark

Transcript—Session 3 with Jake O'Brian.
Conducted by Mark O'Brian-Hicks, MS Psychology.

General comments: Jake is really having a breakthrough. It's
uncomfortable, though. I'm directly involved.

Myself: So, you're surprised everybody knows Christy is pregnant?
Jake: Well, yes.
Myself: Really? You know my wife, right?
Jake: Yeah. (Laughs) Kinda…I just didn't think…
Myself: That she'd blab? Try not to hold it against her. She couldn't
possibly have kept it…
Jake: Well, usually… I've always been the one.
Myself: "The one"?
Jake: Yeah, normally I'm the only one whose secrets she keeps.
Myself: You feel like she broke a trust?
Jake: I guess…I'm just surprised… What did she do, just start calling
people?
Myself; (laughs) No. No, of course not, but she probably mentioned
it to somebody after talking to Christy or it slipped out or
whatever…she's not malicious…for Christ's sake, you know that!

She's your sister.

Jake: Yeah, yeah. It doesn't matter.

Myself: Why not?

Jake: It isn't mine.

Myself: I know that.

Jake: Yes. But I still don't know whose baby it is.

Myself: That is tough.

Jake: ( ) I…I think it's Ben's.

Myself: (Long spate of laughter) No…no…I'm sorry. Jake. Jake seriously. You need help. (Laughter)

Jake: Oh nice. Real professional.

Myself: Well…come on… You should know Ben loves one woman at a time. 'Too well' to quote Shakespeare. He idolizes them! Think of how he was about Grace. And you should see him around Val. Makes me fear for him all over again. Though…I think he'll be okay no matter what now. He's learned some things…

Jake: Okay. Okay. One case at a time.

Myself: Yeah. Gotta be professional. Okay. Jake…Jake, look at me now. Ben did not sleep with Christy. I mean, when could he have even done it?

Jake: They were alone together at the reception.

Myself: ( ) Jake, you mean when she led him off the dance floor?

Jake: Yeah.

Myself: Jake, listen to me. I was standing out in the lobby, had just had a crazy conversation with Jen about Val, and I saw them go into that room off the lobby, you know the one? They called me in. We were all drinking. We all had a few giggles at your expense. Then we all went back into the ballroom.

Jake: Really?

Myself: Really.

Jake: Well, shit.

Myself: Yeah, you came all the way back from Washington for this? What else we got?

Jake: Doubt.

Myself: (   ) Well, Jake O'Brian, welcome to the world the rest of us inhabit.

Chapter 12
Jake at the Airport in Washington

It was Mark. The bastard. So smug. Sitting there with his self assurance in a fucking head shrinking session. Unprofessional. Just unprofessional. Manipulative. He's in charge of the whole deal. Oh, he's slick. People call me a player. He's the slick one…'We had a few giggles at your expense…' the bastard! I'm going to just say it to her. I'm going to find out and then I'm getting back on a plane and I'm going to confront the bastard and then….

Then what? Then kill him? Seriously. What the fuck am I going to do with the knowledge?

"How was your flight?"

And here she is. She looks so innocent. She's the one who definitely is not. She's the one I know for an absolute certainty is not innocent. Or, do I? Why… Why don't I feel mad at her? Maybe the kid is mine!

So cute. So cute.

"Shiny."

"Things go well?""

"Oh, the usual. Shiny."

"You were lucky to get a connecting flight from Poland on such short notice. Glad you didn't need me to interpret. My Polish is rusty."

"No worries, all shiny."

Ask her. Just ask her. You'll be able to tell. He's so smug with his 'Look at me, Jake. Ben did not sleep with Christy' No you bastard, you did, you went off with her right after Ben and Christy had their talk, that's why you know it wasn't Ben, you smug...

She's so cute. So nice to come and get me at the airport. We're... we're together now. Does it matter?

"Traffic heavy?"

"Piece of cake." She kissed him.

What have I been thinking? Did it matter? Did it really matter? Besides, she barely knew Mark. It doesn't matter... But who... Just out of curiosity, who? Or is it all a lie? Just to test me? Just to see if I really love her? Well, if so it worked. I do.

Chapter 13
Sean of the Zipline

So, see my family is crazy. No really. I mean in a good way, mostly, except, except maybe for Christy. Hard to tell. They came out here on a tour with my new Aunt Val. Er...step aunt. What would she be? Anyway, she met my uncle Ben, the poet, professor, semi-famous backwoods artistic genius, not many of those...though, I guess that's not true, that would fit Shakespeare and Twain and Faulkner, except for the 'semi' part... I would love to get back to Shakespeare. I'd love to get back to directing and acting like I started out to do. But, this zipline guiding is fun too, and I'm actually earning a living doing it. Anyway, Aunt Val met Uncle Ben on a train. Yeah, right out of an old movie or something and they fell in love, which is nice because they're both really old and both have had a tough go. Big long story. No time. Got another tour coming.

Anyway, like I said, they're crazy. Aunt Val's a travel agent and she had a tour coming out here, nice midwestern people from Iowa, always fun to put farm folks and folks from up north like I am on the line. Then love it, you know? They're not too cool, not too sophisticated to have fun. They holler and tell jokes and they laugh and they're not trying to fool anybody, you know. They're not ironic. And don't kid yourself, most people who use that word don't even know what it means, including Alanis, but that's another story.

So, my family: crazy. There's Uncle Ben and Aunt Val,

and now there's my aunt, I guess, Christy…more about her
in a minute…and my Uncle Jake who's some kind of big time
government lawyer who travels all around clarifying and writing
and rewriting international law and stuff near as any of us can tell…
always has been a rumor he's a spy. Total crap. Nobody that goofy
could be a spy. "Kiddo." He says "kiddo" and "shiny" like in Firefly,
only I don't think he's ever seen it. Anyway, he's kind of a player and
he's getting pretty old for it. And now he's got Christy… My dad
has something to say about that. More on that later.

Oh, and my mom and dad. They are lovable, but what a
mismatch! Maybe that's why it works. Dad is so low key and calm
that he doesn't get freaked out by anything, not even counseling
guys in a prison. Doesn't bring crazy home at all, though I know
he sees all kinds of crap. He's just, in the best sense, cool. And then
there's Mom… Back home in Hunter, they say if you want to keep
anything secret, don't go within half a mile of the Hicks house.
She used to be a reporter, now she's got a column, and she's got a
book coming out about a guy back there, you may remember the
story, you know, the ex-marine who fought in the Middle East who
saved his own family, including his Afghani grandchildren…

Yeah, that book. And she does a good job with it. First of
all, she doesn't leave out his wife, Carrie Sylvanus…and she goes
easy on all the subplots about priest hostages and… Well, she had
the right touch for the story. Anyway, Mom knows everything
about everybody in town. Uncle Ben says she always has, calls
her "The Little Sneak." Once, when I was about ten, I called her
that 'cause I caught her looking in my drawers for cigarettes or
something… She chased me around the house, and finally we both
started laughing. She's a good sort, but she is a pain sometimes. Well,
she's a mom, I guess.

Anyway, this Christy… Let me tell you there was some
weird crap going on with her this weekend. After I took them up
on the line, not Christy, 'cause she's seven months pregnant, we all
kinda crashed in this nice B and B in the little berg down by the
river, Jake rented the whole thing! The downstairs for Val and her
tour and the upstairs for everybody else. It was pretty cool getting

to see them all, but, the walls are pretty thin in that place and, late at night, I could hear Christy and Val through the one in my bedroom. Val had come up to visit the family and left the tour partying in that great unaffected midwestern way, downstairs. Anyway, Christy took her aside into this room and I was texting my girlfriend, Kat, who was coming over later, with my head up against the wall. That's when I heard Christy tell Val…get this…that my Uncle Ben slept with her at the hotel during her and Uncle Jake's wedding reception and that the baby is actually Uncle Ben's.

"I know this is really hard to hear, but I just wanted you to know because there may be complications, and well, he wasn't being untrue to you, because he didn't know you were there…"

And then I was so proud of my Aunt Val! We had some nice talks back in Hunter last summer, and I got to know her, because she just says aloud in that flat Iowa way just what I was thinking, "Well…that isn't true."

"Oh, I know it's shocking but…"

"It's not shocking, Christy, because it isn't true. I was there, as you know, and I was watching him, and I saw the two of you go off the dance floor and talk to Mark and giggle about Jake and then you all came back into the ballroom."

And then, get this, Christy just starts bawling and she says, "Oh…oh…you're right. It's the hormones…It's…No you're right. It's not Ben's at all. You know, of course, it's Michael's. We were almost married and that night…"

And Aunt Val says, "…and that night Michael and your Uncle Ben got drunk and planned their Mariposa Grove trip. And before that, you hadn't seen Michael, according to what Jen told me, in what…five or six…"

And then I hear my Mom say, because, of course she was listening outside the door, "Now what in the world is this all about…?"

And Christy goes, "Oh…oh…it's the hormones…excuse me. Excuse me. It's so hard to tell you that…"

And my mom goes, "You're going to say it was Mark now…right?"

And Christy goes, "Oh…you don't believe me?"

And Val goes, "Christy. Christy. Here…"

And she must have handed her a hanky or something, and there's crying and then all of a sudden I hear Jake's big booming slick voice going, "Everything shiny in… Oh, Christy. You on a jag again? Oh come here honey…It's okay." And they go off.

And I hear Uncle Ben say, "What is with that girl?"

Then Mom say, "I don't know. Next thing we know she'll say *I'm* the father."

And Val just starts dying laughing and then I hear my dad say, "Shhhh…shhhh…Now it's probably just…"

Mom says, "He's going to say it's because of her 'condition'! Oh gosh, Mark, where's the fainting couch? We weak women just can't cope. We're so glad you big, strong men are here to calm us down. You know, there are pregnant women who could kick your ass, Mark Hicks."

And Uncle Ben says, "Actually there are skinny little sneaks who can kick his ass."

And Mom says, "Shut up, you…"

And then everybody finishes the sentence with, "…you don't know me." That happens whenever we get together. It's an O'Brian family thing. Don't know how it got started. Gotta admit, I like it. It's kind of about how well we know each other. Anyway, after that, everybody laughs really hard.

Then Aunt Val says, "Seriously, what in the world is going on with that girl?"

And Uncle Ben says, "And what in the world is going on with Jake? The player is getting played!"

And Dad says, "I believe it's called karma."

And this kind of rush of air goes through the room like everybody remembering at once all the beautiful girls in Uncle Jake's life for all these years, never any one for more than a month or two.

Dad hit it right on and that was the moment. Like I said, my family: crazy. Crazy smart.

My opinion? I'm with Dad. Uncle Jake had it coming.

Chapter 14
Fun Out West
With Mick and Jane

He was on horseback, out riding the range with his father-in-law, Mick, on their spread outside Reno. Open, just open land. Little dots of buildings here and there in the distance. Could be a mile or seven away, hard to know. He felt the way here that he always did in open country all around the world: out of place. This time there was something new, though. He felt homesick. He wanted to be back in Hunter again. He'd never felt that way before. Nesting? Jesus, who's pregnant?

"Rattler bite your horse?" His father-in-law Mick, up ahead, was wondering why he'd stopped. Mick never stops.

Ten years older than I am and puts me to shame. I'll have to ask him the secret, but I think he'll just grin, and glance out at the open country.

I miss water, when I'm in places like this. I think that's partly it. But I've never missed it so much before. I keep seeing Hunter Lake. I want to be on the shore there, looking out, with Christy. Just be there where my roots are, my family. The one I ran from as fast as I could all those years ago. This is so...well, so not me. Not shiny at all. I'm...well...thinking about things, repercussions, recriminations. And still, still, the whole baby thing. Whose kid is it? Is it really just mine? Is what's going on with Christy all hormonal, or...

"...she's always been like that..."

Those words of Michael's just kept echoing in my mind.

Have I married a female version of myself? Is this how it feels to be on the other side of all those "relationships"?

Back when he was a kid and he and Ben had both been in the Catholic school in Hunter (long since shut down) he remembered talk of Purgatory. It was supposed to be the place where you atoned for your sins before you passed on to Heaven.

Is that where I am now?

"I'm coming, chief," he said to Mick and flashed his Jake smile. "Everything's shiny."

Back at the ranch house Christy and Jane were fixing dinner by now. Jane scared him. She had that regal air of ownership dynastic people of all cultures had. She'd eyed him up the first time she saw him. It was like Mom's look. It said, "Don't mess with me or mine, mister," in no uncertain terms. And truth was, for once, he hadn't. She hadn't needed to warn him. He was ready to be a true husband and he had been.

Well, except for running off from Christy and getting on planes seven or eight times and running around the world in jealous rages and ill-fated detective missions. Jesus, whose kid is it?

He wondered what the talk Christy and her mom were having was like. Tearful? Almost every talk anybody had with Christy right now was tearful. Everything made her cry. Women pushing baby carriages in the park, scruffy dogs playing with equally scruffy little boys and girls. Old married couples holding hands, TV commercials for men's razors. It was getting ridiculous. He hoped Jane would infuse Christy with some of her hardy old toughness. Thing was, Christy had always been tough up to now, if a little spoiled.

Is it all an act?

They had spoiled her, Jane and Mick. There was just no denying it. Any time she wanted anything she just called her mom and it showed up within days. She never asked Jake for anything though Jake had lavished gifts aplenty upon her, including her vintage Porsche. That had not been a small ticket item.

He was jealous. He was truly jealous of every man who

even talked to her. Any of them could be the father of her child. Or again, was it all just a way to control him? Didn't she know he was already controlled? Didn't she know that he was probably more maternal than she was at this point? Couldn't she read it in his eyes? Didn't she know how much he wanted to take her home, back to Hunter, settle down and raise kids? Be a good person for the first time in his life?

No.

No Jake, she doesn't know, because you don't tell her. You just say "Shiny" or some equally stupid thing and go on with your day. You've been playing this character so long there isn't any other you anymore. You ran from Hunter as soon as you could after Dad died and you got the hell away from it all, Mom's controlling hand, Ben's judging eye, even Jen's, my-big-brother-can-do-no-wrong admiration. You made up Jake O'Brian, the player, Jake O'Brian the international lawyer, Jake O'Brian the rake and rambler, Jake O'Brian the maybe spy. Jake O'Brian the enigma. And now, Jake O'Brian you are stuck with him until you find a way to be Jake O'Brian the family man. Until you find a way to be outside, to others, what you are inside.

"I want to go home."

Mick gave him a funny look over his shoulder. "We're headed that way partner."

He had startled himself saying that aloud and had a difficult moment shaking it off. "Yeah. Yeah, I know Mick. What...um... what do you suppose the girls have cooked up?"

"Oh, somethin' rich and good...rich and good...like always. Probably with some peppers in it. Jane learned to work with peppers from Maria Juarez, their cook when she was growin' up. Sometimes, her chilli is even a little too hot for me."

"Must be that Ukranian blood."

"Ha, yeah, cold people I come from. But I'm much removed at this point."

"Yeah," Jake said.

Much removed. That's it. I've removed myself. I've removed myself. Now I need to go back. How do I do that? If I say that to Christy, "Hey, let's just settle down and..." She still wants to travel. We're supposed to be at this honeymoon thing for another few months yet. And how is that going to work with the pregnancy? I hope Jane is talking to her about that. I hope somebody is.

What the hell is going on? Who is talking inside my head? I don't recognize the voice. I want to go home! What I wouldn't give just to have a sit down with Ben, really talk to him for once. Sort this all out. I could talk to Mark again. What was I thinking? I actually thought he might be the father. Mark? I'm cracking up. You know who I really need to talk to? Mom. What would she say?

"Jake, some day you'll have to have a reckoning."

That's exactly what she'd say, because she used to say that every time she saw me. What did she mean by that? What did she mean? This is what she meant.

I'm in Purgatory. That's where I am. The nuns in the Catholic school in Hunter, now long closed, promised it and I'm there. I'm atoning for past sins. I just didn't get it. I thought they were talking about some place floating in some dark region of the ether with demons and pitchforks. So mythological. I used to joke with Ben about it. But, it's not like that, it's more like in Dante. The Italians and Ben made me read the whole Divine Comedy. They insisted I read the whole thing because they didn't want me stuck in the Inferno or the Purgatorio. I read it all just to humor them. Thought the idea that some stupid ancient book could take my "immortal soul" prisoner or something was hilarious Just for kicks, I read most of it in Italian. Well, my Italian friends and Ben were both wrong in one way, because even though I finished it all, I'm stuck anyway. I'm in the middle place in late mid-life on a long rough steep spiral road back to the surface. Okay, I'm here. How do I atone? How do I work my way up?

The old "shiny" part of him wanted so badly not to be thinking this way. Shiny wanted so badly just to ride away right now right back up to the ranch door and laugh it all off. Laugh everything off like he used to. Hang out with Christy for another month or two, or less, and then one evening at an office party, or in a park, in a bar or coffee shop, or on a subway somewhere, just take up with some exotic new girl, seek out a greener pasture in another country somewhere where there are no babies, no commitments, no jealousies, drop Christy a good-natured goodbye note and a few hundred thousand and just go on having fun forever. Where in the hell was that guy who thought that way, or really, didn't think or certainly didn't worry about anything at all? Where was Shiny?

Gone. And he isn't coming back. Shiny is over. I have a wife I love and a child I will love on the way. That's the first thing: Shiny is gone, forever. And good riddance. Time to put away childish things.

"Hey, you okay there, Jake?

"Huh? Oh…shiny." Hard habit to break. This was not going to be easy. "No worries."

"Supper's probably about done by now."

"Well then, race ya back to the ranch, Mick."

"Oh, yer a horseman now?'

"Nope, but I can hang on."

"Okay, let's jump some gullies then."

Jake pulled down his Tigers cap and prepared for the hard ride ahead.

Chapter 15
Home Talk on a Beach in Fiji

"You mean, just stay there? Give up my job?"

"Well, no. Not if you don't want to, but maybe just until the baby is a little older."

Christy was gorgeous as always, cute as a button, even with…maybe especially with her little baby belly, which was getting pretty big. In fact, surprisingly big, Jake thought, as they lay back on the beach. It was a lonely stretch, a place Val had suggested, when Christy had insisted on another trip. Val said the beach might be good for a quiet talk. Fiji. White sand, 78 degrees. Cool Pacific breeze. Nothing but sun. Beautiful. What wasn't beautiful was the 15 hours of vomiting Christy did on the plane. But it was all her idea. She was going to the South Pacific, seven months pregnant. And she was from tough pioneer stock. She seemed stable now, physically.

"I'd have to think about that, Jake. I'd have to think about that a long time. I'm still…well, young."

"And I'm old?"

"Well, no…older than me though." Tears were welling again. "It's such a small town…"

"Oh, now…"

"I'm such a shit. Here the man of my dreams is pouring out his soul…"

"Well it's good…good to know I'm the man of…"

"No, no. Stop with the charm. Listen to me now. This baby, this baby isn't yours, Jake."

"It doesn't matter."

"Doesn't it? If you knew, if you knew…"

He was silent, pensive.

She was waiting for him to ask the question. He didn't completely fear the answer, because no matter what it was it might still be a lie. And no matter what the truth was, he would love this child. What's more, he would love Christy. He knew that. So, there were some benefits to life in Purgatory.   "Do…you want to know?"

"Do you want me to know?" *Jesus, I sound like Mark. Maybe that's a good thing.*

"Don't do that."

"What?"

"Be fatherly."

"Oh…okay." He was quiet. "Shiny…" *Shit.*

"You're working that word pretty hard."

She's right. I can't pretend anymore. I've lost the knack. Fuck it. Fuck pretending.

He looked over at her, and now she saw that he was crying. The look on her face went aghast.

"What do you want me to do, Christy? I'll do it."

"I…I don't know…"

They looked out at the Pacific from the snow-white beach. In all that expanse, the biggest in the world, there were no answers.

That night, Jake got very drunk, while Christy slept. He woke up late and felt the emptiness around him. He could feel before his eyes opened that he was alone in the bed. He listened with his eyes still closed. Then he got up and looked around. The beach house was vacant. He walked out through the sliding doors onto the beach. Then went out back.

Christy was gone.

Chapter 16
Fourth Session With Mark

Transcript—Session 4 with Jake O'Brian. Conducted by Mark O'Brian-Hicks, MS Psychology.

General Comments: Jake is unglued. Just completely unglued. I've never seen him like this. Nobody I know has. I fear for him.

Myself: Okay. Maybe we just innumerate…
Jake: Fuck you! *Innumerate…* This is my life, Mark. Are you getting that?
Myself: That's why we're here.
Jake: Okay…Okay. Sorry.
Myself: Goes with the territory. Now look, first, you know where she is.
Jake: I know where she was. Jane won't tell me where she is.
Myself: Um…Mick won't, either?
Jake: Don't know. He doesn't do phones.
Myself: Doesn't… Never mind. Anyway, you know she's safe and the baby is safe. Jane told you Christy was thinking clearly and had a definite goal in mind. Christy said, in the note she left you, that she wasn't mad at you. She was mad at herself…
Jake: But she doesn't want to see me.
Note: Jake was clutching the note like a lifeline. I wonder how long he'd been holding it.

Myself: Right. I was getting to that…

Jake: Why doesn't she want to see me? For Christ's sake! I'm okay with the baby not being mine…

Myself: Are you?

Jake: Well…Jesus…no, I'm not. No, I'm not happy. But I'll live with it as long as I can be with her. Jesus! For once, I'm the injured party here. Doesn't anybody fucking know that I'm the fucking injured party here?! (Tears.)

Myself: Jake. Now take a breath. Think about this. Why would you want to be with her?

Jake: To make sure she's safe.

Myself: Her mother told you she was. Do you not trust Jane?

Jake: Of course. She and Mick are salt of the earth…

Myself: Okay, so she's safe. So that reason is out. What else is there?

Jake: Well, I love her, and she's my wife.

Myself: Yes, but she doesn't want to see you right now.

Jake: Or maybe ever. Mark, Mark…if I don't see her again, I don't think I'll make it. I *have* to see her again. I'll…I'll die if I don't. I really think I will. Christ…how did I get like this? I don't want to be like this. I've always tried to make sure that I'd never be like this. It's too fucking hard!

Myself: Jake. Jake. Breathe. Did she say that? Did she say she never wanted to see you again?

Jake: No.

Myself: Did Jane say that?

Jake: No.

Myself: So?

Jake: So…what?

Myself: So that's not on the table. You're going to see her again.

Jake: Okay. Okay. That's a little better. Yeah.

Myself: Now, what did you want to see her for?

Jake: What kind of a fucking question is…

Myself: Humor me.

Jake: I don't know. To tell her I love her.

Myself: Does she know that?

Jake: Yes.

Myself: How many times have you told her that lately?

Jake: Oh…God. With every breath.

Myself: Jake, when you were in your player stage, what drove you away from women fastest?

Jake: Are you saying Christy's a player?

Myself: No. But think. What drove you away from women fastest?

Jake: Yeah…okay. Their saying "I love you," being clingy, was like opposite poles: magnet to magnet.

Myself: And do you think that right now, if you were with her, telling her that you love her "with every breath…" Do you think doing that some more would help?

Jake: Okay…Okay I get you, but I would just like to see her…

Myself: Why?

Jake: Maybe, maybe I could talk some sense into her.

Myself: By saying what?

Jake: I don't know.

Myself: What did you say to her in Fiji?

Jake: Oh…God…That I wanted to bring her back to Hunter and raise the baby there.

Myself: And what was the result?

Jake: She went to bed, I got drunk, and when I woke up in the morning she was gone.

Myself: So, wherever she is, as long as you know she's safe, what's probably the best thing to do?

Jake: Let her come back to me. Get busy with something else. Go back to Washington and work, I guess. But that's just it. I don't want to do that job anymore. I want to raise the kid. I want to be with Christy.

Myself: Well Jake, that's not going to happen right now.

Jake: (   ) I know. What the hell do I do?

Myself: Cope.

Jake: How? How? I've never been good at that. I…I'm shitty at it, really. After Dad died, I got out of that house as soon as I could.

Myself: Well, Jake, you were eleven. You didn't leave for seven years.

Jake: I buried myself in sports until I could leave. Everybody was sad there. I couldn't stand it.

Myself: You wanted to keep things shiny.

Jake: Yeah…funny.

Myself: Being in sports was a nice way to honor your dad. A nice way to remember him. He would have been proud.

Jake: You think?

Myself: If it were your son, wouldn't you be? All state in two sports, all that? Wouldn't that make you proud?

Jake: Yes. Yes, I guess so, but I was just doing it because it was fun. It was all so easy. I wasn't honoring Dad.

Myself: But you did anyway. And even if you weren't thinking of that at the time, you were just a kid. Cut yourself some slack.

Jake: So was Ben. And Jen was even younger, and they just stayed there and took the full hit. And they looked out for Mom until she died. And then the awful thing with Grace. Those two and the kids, they carried the whole load and I…I…

Myself: You were there, too.

Jake: Oh sure, wrapping up the legal stuff. Shiny.

Myself: That's what you were equipped to do.

Jake: "Equipped"? What am I, a fire truck? "Equipped."

Myself: Jake, okay, I'll grant you this. You have been a shit.

Jake: A huge shit.

Myself: Okay, a big steaming pile sometimes, but you've done an awful lot of good with what you've made of…

Jake: Oh, bullshit! All that stuff with those governments, all my legal work and building of whatever it is I've built doesn't make me any less a shit. When the chips are down with the people I love… Oh God, just ask Ben and Jen and Kate and Michael and… Jesus… you. Grace died, and I just took off. Left you all, so I could go fuck super models.

Myself: That was a long time ago.

Jake: Yeah, but I did that. Showed up for the funeral, for the legal stuff, and then just left, off to my fucking shiny life again. Left my brother to cope with all that alone.

Myself: He was hardly alone…

Jake: No, no. Thanks to you guys. But not thanks to me. I'm…I'm a shit, Mark.

Myself: What if you are?

Jake: What?

Myself: What if you are? Can you change? Will regret and worry and self- recrimination change what's happened in the past one tiny bit?

Jake: No. No… Okay. No. Happy?

Myself: Are you?

Jake: I'm fucking miserable!

Myself: And going back to work, or running to work, isn't the answer this time?

Jake: No.

Myself: So you feel like you want to come back here. Set down some roots.

Jake: Yes.

Myself: And you've got the money? And the firm is set to run without you for the next six months anyway, since you and Christy were going to be on the grand tour…

Jake: Yeah. Money is not the problem. And I've got a little time.

Myself: Then, why not do it? Come back here, I mean. The cabin next to…

Jake: Yeah, yeah I know. I was looking at that.

Myself: So? Why not rent it?

Jake: So, maybe… Renting is just pouring money away. I'll buy the fucker. Why not? I can afford it.

Myself: Yes. Why not?

Jake: Then what?

Myself: Then wait. See what happens. Let Christy come to you. Or not…

Jake: I don't like that last part. What if she…

Myself: Life is risk, Jake. There are no guarantees.

Jake: That simple? Really? Buy the place. Wait. See what happens.

Myself: Well…hardly simple. But it seems the most logical thing to do.

Jake: What, what if she never comes?

Myself: I'm…I'm not going to lie, Jake, that *could* happen.

Jake: Oh God. Even if she does. Until then… What will I do?

Myself: Well, it's hunting season.

Jake: Think Ben would take to that?

Myself: One way to find out.

Chapter 17
On Huck's Island With Jake

Duck hunting with Jake is never any fun. Mostly, that's for two reasons. First, he's a great shot. Second, he doesn't care about duck hunting. It's the same way now as it was when we were kids. We go out, set up, first duck that goes by he shoots easy as pie with one shot. It's that hand/eye coordination stuff. Same thing that made him a great athlete.

He shoots a duck, even two, on one pass. Then he looks at me and starts talking about sports or his latest case or in the old days every woman he's ever slept with and there have been a lot of them… whatever… as if he hadn't just done something great by dropping two birds with one shot, three with two, whatever.

I'd kill to be able to shoot like he can and he doesn't even care. That's maybe why he hits them so easily: it's a given he's going to and he doesn't care if he doesn't.

And this time, this time is worse really. It's worse because he's still just blabbing away but this time he's beside himself, even crying sometimes. I've never seen him like this. But still, he's dropping every duck that passes: two drake buffleheads and a mallard hen to my single bluebill drake, and this time, between brilliant, uncanny shots, the greatness of which he doesn't even acknowledge, he's blabbing about Christy. And when it's not about Christy, he's apologizing for all the shit he did or didn't do in the past. He's big on sin of omission. I'm going to send him to talk to

Father Bill, I think. I hope Father sends him on a pilgrimage to Lourdes.

"I'm so sorry, Ben."

"You said that."

"Yeah, but I am."

"Jake, it was a long time ago. Oh…here come…nope, mergansers."

"We don't shoot those?"

"Never have. How can you not know that?"

"Don't know. Just never thought of it… Shiny. But… anyway…I should have been there, for you guys. After Grace and with Mom."

"Jake, we've discussed this over and over. I know you feel bad, but we can't change what's happened."

"I would if I could."

"I know. If you want me to beat you up for it some more, I will. It was heartless what you did, both times. 'You just took care of the papers and left us.' That's the way you put it earlier, right? That what you want to hear?"

"I said that?"

"Yeah, about fifteen minutes ago, and an hour before that, and in the big boat on the way across the big lake, and in the canoe paddling down here."

The one good thing about having Jake along is that Tom, my young chocolate lab, gets a lot of work. Ducks dropping everywhere. He's having a ball just getting airborne off the bank. Happy lab fun. He loves Jake. All the sporting types do: men, women, children, dogs.

Earlier in the year, Jeff Jesson and I brought Huck, my old veteran lab out, too, just so the old guy could watch the fun, but we couldn't keep him from going in the water. It got cold that day, too, trace ice, and he just blasted in there when Tom was reluctant once. So, now he stays home. I mean, come on, he's almost 15 years old! And he's coming off a massive stroke that would have killed any other dog. When I leave him at camp now, there has to be somebody there with him, or he'll howl across the lake calling for me. It's not forlorn. It's more like communication: "Hey, chum, what is the deal? You forgot me! Come back here! You can't do the job without me." Today, Val is there spoiling him. The old guy still likes the ladies. She's probably feeding him pancakes by now. Apparently pancakes, or "puppy cakes" as the kids used to call them when they'd feed Huck from the table against my orders, are better than hunting to that old dog's mind.

The sunrise was great this morning, off beyond the wrap-around pond behind this muddy finger of Hunter Lake. Gorgeous: oranges, pinks, purples, blue horizontal clouds. Came up like a really great recurring dream. You're just so glad it's back.

Jake didn't even comment on it other than to say, "Shiny" when I pointed it out. That word is rarely literal with him. Here we are, sitting on the seats of the old family canoe, on a little island we've hunted on since we were boys, and named after the island in *Huck Finn*. Here we are, brothers, in the fifth decade of our lives. Together, watching a sunrise on the lake where my dad planted roots all those years ago and Jake just doesn't even notice. That's the thing. Jake doesn't look at the world he's in. He's made a habit of being two steps ahead of everybody else for so long, that he can't enjoy anything if it's not a game. It's always all been a game to him. The goal is to never take anything seriously. And, to be fair, in a way, it's always worked for him. The thing is that he just isn't aware. He has just made himself so hard, or just unconscious from what I can tell, that he doesn't notice things that matter. It's always the next thing with him. That's why this is so hard for him, I think. There is no next thing, only the waiting.

"What…what should I do now?"

"You mean other than shooting all the ducks on the lake?"

"What? Oh. I don't have to shoot, Ben. I'm just out here because you like it."

"Jake, that is not a good way to make up for past hurts."

"What isn't?"

"Patronizing people."

"Am I…"

"I swear, how in the hell did you ever cut a deal with

anybody? How did you negotiate and arbitrate all that language with all those politicians and bureaucrats?"

"Political types like to be patronized, I guess. They expect it. They aren't as smart, as discerning as you."

"Well, like I said, quit patronizing me…I'm your brother, not some third world political asshole you're trying to cut a deal with or some hot woman on the make looking for a compliment, and I fucking hate to be patronized. Clear?"

"You know, you communicate very well. That's a gift bro'." He grins at me. Touch of the old Jake.

"Knock it off. You want to go back and watch football or something?"

"No, I want to hunt with you."

"Fine. Then shut up or talk about sports or something."

"Fine."

"And there is one thing you could do for me, Jake."

"Name it."

"Miss."

"Wouldn't I be patronizing you then?"

"Yes, but that would be okay."

"How will you know when I'm missing for real and when I'm patronizing you?"

"Thanks. Well, that's out now too. Go ahead. Shoot them all."

"Seriously. I do like this. I like it because it's now."

"As opposed to 'then'?"

"Yeah."

"There's nothing you can do about the past that does any good, Jake."

"And the only thing I can do about the future is wait… Tell me again."

"No."

"Just once more."

"Okay, but this is the last time. I never slept with Christy… God it's a joke to even think that…she wouldn't… A fat old English teacher… It's ridiculous."

"You're not fat anymore. You look great. Tell me again. Humor me."

"Okay. If I have to, but quit telling me how good I look. Am I supposed to look bad? I've had 16 people ask me if I'm on chemo."

"Says something about America I guess. Somebody gets skinny, they must be sick. Anyway, that's not flattery. You do look good. Now…please…tell me once more about you and Christy."

"Shit. Okay. There is no me and Christy. There never was. I never did sleep with her, or even kiss her other than a peck on the cheek at the wedding. And Mark never did either."

"You know that for…"

"I know that for certain, because if he had, Jen would have his nuts hanging on a pole in the front yard. Now are we done with this?"

"And Michael?"

"Michael was getting drunk with me that night. He hadn't slept with her since they split and she took up with you. I wish I didn't know about that. You're lucky I didn't kill you. Good thing I didn't know at the time."

"Well, I thought I should tell you now. Full confession."

"I always thought that sacrament was overrated. Now are we done with this?"

"Yes."

"Really?"

"No."

"That's what I thought. Well, whatever you need. I hope it all works out, Jake, but if it doesn't…"

"Yeah?"

"You're going to have to deal with that too. How's the remodeling going?"

"Pretty good. I've had Dale over and Mr. Sylvanus… John… too. They do great work."

"Yes. They do. If you get John involved it gets done on time too."

"Ben?"

"Yeah?"

"Life is hard."

"You think?"

Chapter 18
Family Meeting at the Camp

"What are we going to do about him?" Jen sighed. She looked over the counter at the family gathered around the table on the front porch. Ben, his daughter Kate, her husband David, Jen's husband Mark, and her son Collin, home for the weekend.

Mark rubbed at his whiskers, "There's not much more we can do, hon. He's just going to have to tough it out."

Jen angrily flipped a pancake on the ancient griddle. "I'm trying to finish the Dale book and he's in my face every 15 minutes!"

"What's the title, again?" Ben asked.

"A Mixed Up and Splendid Rescue."

"Yeah, yeah I like it more all the time. Reference to Twain and it covers the story. It really is a great story."

"You couldn't make it up. Having a hard time with the publishers because they think the title is too long."

"Don't they know Twain? Jesus. The great unwashed. It's a great title, Jen."

"Whoa! A compliment from Ben to Jen!" Kate said, laughing.

"Shut up, you…" Ben said grinning.

Everybody chimed in with, "…you don't know me!"

"Anyway," Jen said, "I can't get fifteen minutes worth of work done and he's standing next to me. That's the thing that's the worst. He just comes in. Doesn't knock… He's just standing there smiling pathetically… Maybe he is a spy."

"Nobody that goofy could be a spy," Kate said. "You want some help, Aunt Jen… I can…"

"No, thanks sweetie. I've got it."

It was Kate's turn to sigh, "I know about the showing up stuff. He does that at our house too. Woke Dave up out of a sound sleep…"

David Loonsfoot smiled, "Ah, it's okay. I sleep enough in the back at the grocery."

Collin laughed, pulling back his long messy blond hair. Then he grinned at his old assistant football coach as he launched an attack, "I'd say you do get your share in all right. You used to sleep in the coach's office."

David looked at his old right side linebacker, "Shut up, you…"

Everyone chimed in, delighted that David had joined the family game. "You don't know me."

Jen thought about that old saying. It had started when they were kids. She and Ben always argued about the origin. He claimed Dad had originated it in talking to Mom. Jen maintained it was a clever little something she'd uttered as a kid. The argument would never stop. She smiled and flipped another pancake.

"Seriously, though," she said. "I've got a deadline. Can't we keep him busier with the new camp?"

"Dale and John are almost done. Probably will be by the time he gets back from…where is he?"

"Manilla," Jen said. "At least that's what he said."

"Think he's looking for Christy?" Kate asked. "She doesn't want to see him. She called me last week from somewhere. She wouldn't tell me where. It's weird. I hardly know her really, and she talks to me like we're old friends. Confides all this stuff."

"Like what?"

"Jen," Mark said, "if she told you it wouldn't be confiding anymore…"

"This is serious, Mark," Jen snapped back.

"It's okay…" Kate said. "There's nothing new to tell. She slept with everybody… She feels bad. She's been unfair to Jake. Poor Jake…boo hoo…"

"Now, Kate. You're not being fair. "

"Dad, I don't know what that girl would do if she had some of the shit happen to her that's happened to us."

Mark nodded. "You're right. But everybody deals with what they have to deal with, or doesn't, and we all just need to be kind."

"Oh, thank you, Dr. Feelgood…" Ben said.

Mark looked over at Ben and laughed. "See what I mean?"

Ben cackled.

"Shut up, you…" Jen started.

"You don't know me." Everyone finished.

Ben looked around at everyone. "Well, we do need a plan. Val is coming again next week and I'm hoping to have some time alone."

"Good luck with that," Kate said. "Even if Jake wasn't suddenly appearing."

Ben shook his head, "The last time Val was here, we were out on the porch, and he did that appearing thing. I said to Val, 'Lo, look where the apparition comes…' I don't think he got it. Never big on the classics."

"You and Val have any big plans in the offing?" Jen said as she brought in the pancakes.

"Oh, lord… Stop pushing that button, Jen! We like it just the way it is. Val has her business and her family in Iowa, and until she gets some of that sorted out… Hey, wait… I could move to Iowa for the duration of Jake's woes and…"

"Don't you dare! I'm not dealing with that dope alone!" Jen said. "And think about your daughter! She'd have to nursemaid him too."

"Just trying to see you get all riled," Ben grinned. "It worked too. You're not doing the marriage talk anymore."

"Doofus!"

"Sneak!"

Mark took a drink of coffee, set it down and looked around the table. "Well, this is fruitful. So…what's the plan?"

Ben laughed. "I could go over to his camp and have Dale and Sam break a few things. Or I could tell them to nail the doors shut with Jake inside once they're finished. We could make a food slot. Visit him once a week."

"Be serious, Ben." Jen said walking back into the kitchen tossing one pancake each to Huck and Tom as she passed.

"You're spoiling them rotten."

"Oh like you don't, doofus."

"Food Looks great, hon," Mark said.

"Mark, have you thought about having some sessions with him?" Ben asked.

"I…"

Ben looked over at Mark and read the expression. "Okay… sorry… professional courtesy officially in order. Next subject."

"What?" Jen said, then examined Ben's expression. "Oh… oh…they're already…oh. Yeah, I knew that."

"Yeah, unfortunately." Mark said.

"He told me himself, Mark."

"Enough said."

"Okay," said Kate. "So there's that. How do you get the pancakes to cook so evenly with that old griddle. I always burn them using that. Always did."

"We ate them anyway," Ben said. "And the dogs got extra."

"Shut up you!" said Kate.

"You don't know me," said everyone.

They ate in silence for a while, passing the homemade syrup, "Camp Grossy Maple" read the label. "Finest syrup made in the Gros Rocher Swamp".

"Ray's got a good batch this year," Mark said.

"Yup," said Ben. "Some of the best ever. He's getting all scientific now. He goes on and on. Almost like listening to Jake, except he doesn't whine."

"So, you and Val…no serious plans…" Jen said from the kitchen.

"Oh, for God's sakes! You'll be the first to know!"

"You'll tell me then?"

"No, but you'll still be the first to know."

Everyone laughed loud and long.

Mark finally said, "And, on the whole Jake issue, I'm afraid there's no easy answer. We're just going to have to be patient. See him through it. Whatever happens."

"So," said Kate, "the spy games continue, huh?"

"I never thought I'd see him like this," Ben said. "Really, never. Once he got married, I thought we'd hardly ever see him again. They both travel so much."

"And now he's maybe coming back to settle here." Jen said. "No…no, you're right, this is a side I've never seen."

Ben was truly surprised, "Really? You two have always been so close."

"Yeah, but he never had anything private to say until now. All he ever did was brag and grin about whatever unearthly, bulimic, super model bimbo he was currently 'dating'…" She made air quotes.

Kate choked on some pancake, took a quick drink of coffee.

The laughing began again.

"Shiny," Ben said, when he caught his breath, and the laughs continued.

Chapter 19
Christy and Jane

"You can't hide out here forever, baby." Jane said, looking up from her embroidery from her spot
on the bunkhouse porch swing.

"You didn't tell him I was here, did you, Ma?"

"I told him you weren't staying with us, which is true. You're not up at the house. He knows you're safe, but I've gotten fifteen calls from that sister of his."

"Oh, Jen. She's a pest."

"She's just lookin' out for family. I respect that." Jane looked out over the long range towards the sunset. It had been unseasonably hot that day. Bad weather coming soon though. She could feel it and Mick had confirmed it this morning. "It's gonna get chilly out here soon for a girl with a baby. Well…two babies."

"I know."

"You've got to tell him the truth, Christy."

"I know."

"When he gets that house done."

"It's a shack. I've seen it."

"Now Jake is a good man…"

Christy laughed, "Yeah. Who knew?"

"What do you mean?"

"When I was first dating him even his family warned me about what a rambler he is… Even Michael."

"Now, baby, I don't want to hear any more about that swift transfer from that nice young man to Jake. No more. That was your call and your doing. You own up…"

"Okay. Okay… you're right. You're right."

"If you got yourself a rich playboy, well, he doesn't seem that way anymore. And now you're going to have to be the girl I know you are…"

"Okay Ma. It's just all happening so fast."

"And I'm sure he's got that 'shack' as you call it all fixed up for you. For a baby, the babies. Air tight and snug against the cold. That's what this Jennifer says, anyway."

"You don't know how cold it gets up there, Ma!"

"Neither do you. Guess you'll have to find out."

"Isn't there…something else I could do?"

"Now just what are you suggesting, baby girl?"

"Well, couldn't I live here, raise the twins here?"

"And what, Jake comes for a visit? He's their father, not some rich uncle. And I doubt he'd like being out here, a man like him, under our thumb."

"They're not really his…"

"What?!"

"Well…Ma…I have something to tell you."

Jane set aside her embroidery. Her eyes narrowed. "What?"

"The babies, well… The night of the wedding, I was a little tipsy…"

"Go on…"

"And Jake's brother Ben was a little tipsy and well… we kind of got carried away by a dance, and we headed off upstairs…"

Jane gasped, "Christine Jane Mikoczeski! That is a damned lie! That nice brother of Jake's! You're talking about the poet? The professor?"

Christy nodded, terrified…

"That kind man who made that charming, literate, touching toast at your wedding did not sweep you off your feet like some suave cave man and drag you off to his lair. You take that back this instant!"

Christy's lip trembled. "Okay…okay…it's a lie. It was the psychologist, Jen's…"

"Christy. If you tell one more lie, I will walk out of this bunkhouse and never come back, and you can figure it out all on your own. I don't doubt that the babies aren't Jake's. God knows, I wish I did…" She paused for a moment caught by a thought. "Oh, my God, are they Michael's?"

Christy nodded, her mother's eyes narrowed, and Christy started to cry and shook her head. "No…not Michael's."

"All right darlin', but if they're not Jake's or Michael's, and they're certainly not the spawn of either of those fine gentlemen you tried to besmirch. Whose are they?" Another thought struck. "You didn't tell their wives…girlfriends…whatever…that they were…?"

Christy nodded slowly.

"Oh, Christy…And what did they say?"

"They didn't believe it either." Christy burst into violent tears.

Jane, picked up her embroidery, blew a long breath through her nose and walked back into the bunkhouse, out the back door, mounted up on Climate, her gelding, and didn't stop until she had covered the full mile-and-a-half to the ranch house.

Mick was washing up at the sink near the front porch when she rode up.

"Have a good talk with her?"

Jane, who had been fixating on her daughter's situation, looked Mick squarely in he eye. "Mick, we've raised a crazy person."

He took off his old black stetson and spat out a chew, "Well, we've known that a while. Must come from the mother's side."

"Don't you start with me, Mick," Jane said, half laughing, half scowling.

"She'll be all right. Just let her be."

At the bunkhouse, Christy was still seated on the porch swing. She had stopped crying. "Jake will kill him if he finds out," she said aloud.

How am I going to fix this?

Chapter 20
Christy Comes to Hunter Lake

"Twins?"

Christy bit her lip and nodded.

I don't know whether to believe her. Is she lying? If she is, does she know she's lying? Whose twins are they?

"Why didn't you tell me before? You've known for months, right?"

Christy nodded.

"Do you know the sexes?"

"Doctor thinks, one of each, but he's not sure."

"So not identical... Wow..."

She looked around the little cottage. He really had fixed it up for her and the babies.

Who knew Jake was a sweet man?

She thought back to when she first met him. She'd seen him as a meal ticket really. He was so sophisticated. So worldly. She would never have guessed he came from such a small town, if she hadn't known it ahead of time. She remembered her thought process then: Michael was never going to have any money, and when she'd found out she was pregnant that other time, and not by Michael, she'd just been well...distraught. She'd needed some help, and Michael, handsome and intriguing as he was, was not a good source for aid and comfort. And so, she'd taken up with Jake, but then the false positive... And she'd been relieved, but she had

Jake by then anyway. And it was a pretty good deal, and she did feel a true affection for him. It was hard not to. And then, right out of the blue, he changed on her… Became…what…maternal. And this other boy. This sweet oh-so-juicy, so young, other boy was right there… Like Jake probably was 24 years ago.

All Ma had said when she heard about the pregnancy was, "Christy, have you never heard of birth control?"

But it's always so hard to remember. And the other ways are such a hassle.

She hadn't said that to Ma, of course. Ma might have slapped her for that, even though she'd never slapped her before. The one thing Ma didn't cotton to was irresponsibility. She hated talking to Ma. Ma knew her. There was a little wiggle room with ol' Mick, but not Ma. Never Ma.

"The cottage looks very nice, Jake."

"We could have a house in town, too. Anything you want."

"Oh…oh…will we live here all year round?"

"You want to live somewhere else? There's a good school here. We could go back to Washington. Whatever you want."

"No. No, I think I might be done translating."

"Oh? Well…we'll have to tell Bump."

"Yes, Bump."

"And where do you want us to live?"

"I don't…I don't…out west maybe…I don't know. Let's talk about something else."

"What?"

He's so frustrating to deal with now. So, so fixated. So…earnest.

"I don't know. I just….oh, Jake…" She started to cry.

"Oh, not again. "

"I'm sorry. I'm sorry. You're just so sweet and I'm asking so much… And…and… if you knew the truth!" She shrieked and started sobbing.

"Lord. Christy, how many times do I have to tell you that it doesn't matter. I don't care if they're the mailman's. They're ours. They're ours together, and I'll do anything to make it all okay. And when you're ready to tell me whose they are, I'll…I'll be fine with it. But don't start with all that stuff about them being Ben's or Mark's or Michael's again. I know that's not true."

"Okay," she said. "Okay. But let's get this over with."

Here it comes, he thought.

"They're…they're *yours.* They're yours." She started crying again. "I was, oh it was the pregnancy, I felt so insecure, like you would take off on me, so…so I told you they were somebody else's just to test you, just to see…"

Jake grinned from ear to ear, "Shiny! Oh, just shiny! I wondered…I wondered if that's what it was. Oh, Christy! I'm not going anywhere unless you want me to. We can raise them here or there, or anywhere you want, but let's…let's start here with all the family around. Jen and Kate and even Val, they'd love to help you.

"Oh…oh…they all hate me. They think I'm an awful person for all the lies…"

"Oh, Christy. That's not true. Whoever I love, they love. My God, they love me, and I've given them reason enough not to. Besides, it's been a crazy time. You're having twins. I mean God knows what that's done to your emotions. It's…it's understandable. They'll just forget about all that nonsense. They already have."

"Oh…oh, I can't imagine how that could be."

"I've been a shit. A shit to everybody. Even you. My God, I left them when they were in the worst kind of need, I left you when I found out you were pregnant. You still love me. They still love me. They're certainly not going to hold a couple of errant words against you. Oh, now don't cry…"

"Oh," she said crying. "You're the most wonderful man in the world."

He kind of is, but he's so different. So changed.

Jake teared up and took her into his arms. "Oh, Christy, it's going to be fine. Just fine. We're going to raise the babies and it's going to be fine…"

Yes…I think, maybe. Maybe it will be.

Part II
For The Long Haul

November 27

By the end of a warm November, Jake and Christy were comfortably settled into the cottage next door to the O'Brian camp. The births were scheduled. There would be a planned C-section on December 10. They received daily visits from Katie and Jen, and by the end of the month, Christy's mother, Jane, was a permanent fixture.

Jake spent a good deal of his time at the family camp, driving Ben half around the bend and even annoying unusually unflappable Val during his visits there.

"Hello, Jake," Val said from her spot watching the sunset on the front porch. "Ben's out in the canoe, searching for the last duck on the lake."

"Oh, I'll wait. Beer in the fridge?"

The sigh in Val's response was nearly inaudible. "Sure, help yourself."

"Hey, Huck! How's the boy?"

"Oh, he just keeps strolling along. Ben says he's never seen anything like it. Jeff Jesson was over here giving him the once over, too. He just shook his head and said Huck was clearly descended from Methusula's string of labradors."

"Yup. Shiny, all right. Hey, boy?"

Huck wagged his tail slowly and looked at Val.

"Ben might be a while."

"Well, that gives us a chance to catch up then."

"I just saw you yesterday, Jake."

"A lot can happen in 24 hours."

"Did it?"

"Nope. Just Jane doing embroidery, not talking to Christy, Christy staring out the window not talking to Jane. Jen visiting and talking for everyone, while Kate tends to Christy's every need."

"That's where they were when I visited the last time. No progress, huh?"

"On the Jane and Christy front? Nope."

"What's that about?"

"Don't know. Don't ask."

"Why not?"

"Don't want to find out."

It occurred to Val that this change that was supposedly coming over Jake was not all that pronounced.

"There's some chips in the cupboard…"

"Already found them." Jake threw himself down in the old leather chair in the west corner of the porch. "What's new with you, Val?"

"Not much. Another tour coming up next week."

"Where?"

"Train they call the City of New Orleans."

"Bet that song gets old on the route."

Val smiled briefly. "You have no idea. Used to like it until I took these tours."

"Never got train travel. Hot and boring if you ask me."

Val's smile wavered only slightly. "Didn't. Oh, here comes the old man…"

Jake stood and turned. He opened the window. "Yup."

"What yup?"

"He's singing, 'Star of the County Down.'"

Huck, who was now seated looking out the window, began to howl.

Val laughed and said, "Oh, yeah. He's pretty good isn't he, boy?" Val stroked the old dog's head.

"Ben's had lots of practice. Everybody on the lake knows the words, just from hearing the old guy singing it in the canoe."

"Best song…" Val started, watching Ben draw nearer.

"…in the world. I know. He always says that," Jake said, smirking.

"I know he does. He's not wrong." Under her breath, she added, "When *he* sings it."

God, she loves him! Thought Jake, who had heard Val's whispered comment.

"I don't know. Heard that song too much," he said aloud.

Ben was turning over the canoe down on the beach by

this time and Tom, the young lab, was sniffing around in the brush. Huck, who had insisted at the door, and was let out by Val, was now inspecting Ben, Tom, and the canoe, which he promptly raised his leg on, marking his property. Jake yelled out the window, "Beer?"

"Jesus, you here again? Go see your wife!"

"I've seen her."

"Look closer."

"Tried that. She tells me to quit staring."

"Jake says he's sick of the song," Val said from the doorway.

"What song?"

"Star of the…"

"Oh, I was singing?"

"Yes you were, babe."

Jake couldn't help noticing the delight in that 'babe' either. Val and Ben were truly in love. Solid, palpable, undeniable middle-aged love, as though they'd known each other 40 years. How did that work? He could barely get a smile out of Christy lately. What would it take? What was going on with her? What was going on with her and her mother? So much feminine stuff at the other building. Add Jen and Kate in, and you had a feminist movement. Val was, well, Val. No nonsense that was for sure. She was really quite fetching, but he'd never really even thought of trying her out. Though it had occurred to him that, just for Ben's sake, just to see if she was…interested…. Just to make sure that Ben could trust her, he might… Oh, who was he kidding? Shiny was dying hard. But Val was too near his own age to fall for his stuff anyway. And he still had an ache in his testicles from where he'd once tried with Grace, and she'd promptly punched him where it counts. Val, was, as everybody noticed, quite a bit like Grace. He bet the right upper cut wouldn't be any different.

Besides, he already knew she wouldn't be interested. He also knew that if he tried, she would tell him to stop, then turn to Ben at the first opportunity and tell him his brother was putting the moves on her. She'd actually said exactly those words as a joke once when he'd made a flirty comment and Ben, who was sitting there reading Shakespeare or some such as usual, and only half heard, had shot him a look that would have stopped a black bear at the bait pile. One thing about Ben, you didn't want to fuck around with a girl he liked. For one, the girls he liked, like Val and Grace, were usually tough, and didn't need his help anyway. What was it about him and tough women? Ben always seemed to pick out somebody like Mom. *Always.* Jake never did.

Huh, what does that say about me?

Anyway, even though he was 60, and not as strong as he once was, and skinnier by close to 70 pounds, Ben still had that Irish temper. He'd "see the black" and tear you a new one before you could turn around. It was still a legend at Hunter High, where Ben had taught before his work at the college. He'd picked up two boys by the back of the neck, neither of them was small, and both of them later ended up in prison, and hurled them out of his classroom one day, when they were screwing around teasing an honor student girl.

Anyway, Val was off limits. He didn't try. He didn't try much these days. Didn't want to. What had happened? Once it had been so easy. Now, well now, he didn't seem to have the energy, or the desire. So, while Shiny was dying hard, he was dying, slowly but surely. Things *were* changing. Women were changing. Was it a good thing that most women were becoming more and more like Mom all the time? Or had they always been that way, and he'd just never noticed. Just naturally gravitated towards the weakest ones in the herd. For sure the prettiest. Then, again, until now he'd never been with any of them long enough to really know them. Could it be that they'd been using him, too, all along? Come on, he'd known that all along, hadn't he? Or was his ego just so big he'd ignored it? And what about Christy? Was she still at it, even now? Even eight months pregnant? Was she playing him for an old fool? How could he know for sure? If they stayed together, he'd find out. Oh, God, they had to stay together! Would he ever know, if she was honest, until the truth just dropped on him like an anvil in an old Road Runner cartoon one day? She wouldn't leave him now, would she?

"Look, Val, Jake's having a thought."

Ben was standing in front of him drinking a beer, then

walked over to hang his camouflage hunting coat on the coatrack in the corner of the porch. His over/under Browning was broken down on the edge of the table, ready for cleaning.

"A couple actually, I think," Val said, smirking.

"Down the usual track?" Ben asked.

"Not the usual, just the most recent." Jake said. "No worries. Shiny."

"Oh God. You got me sleeping with Christy again? Well, I didn't. Right, Val?"

"No Jake, he didn't sleep with Christy, before or after the wedding. And how do we know this?"

"Because you're still with him, Val." Jake said.

"That's a boy."

Ben and Val walked hand-in-hand out the porch door and down to the lake. It had been crazy weather lately. Like late September. Ben and Val were so in love. Well, they were entitled. To what was he entitled? A happy life? Or was there such a thing as entitlement? Shiny was dying. He certainly would never have had these thoughts. He honestly did not remember ever worrying about anything this much. He should just out and ask her if the babies were really his, get it over with once and for all. He'd wait until after they were born, though. But if he asked her again, how would he know she wasn't lying? Did she even know when she was lying? How long could he keep going down this track before he left the rails?

He tried to imagine a scene ten years from now, with the babies ten years old, going in and out the summer slammers at the lake house, Christy calling out to them brightly as she went about her day and himself coming in from the office with a cup of coffee in his hand, then maybe going out the door after the kids with a baseball and gloves. It faded on him. It faded very fast and was replaced by a vision of a little foreign car, driven by Christy, driving away on the lake road, with the kids staring at him out the back window as the car disappeared around the corner and into the trees.

December 16

The babies were born without serious incident as scheduled on December 10. A boy, seven pounds three ounces: Benjamin Marcus O'Brian. Ben was already calling him "BMark." Jake liked it. A girl, six pounds ten ounces: Jane Michelle O'Brian to be known as, "Mikie," after Christy's father. Actually, it wasn't completely without incident. There had been 16 hours of unexpected labor which began just before the planned C-section. "Oh, perfect," Christy had said when her water broke. And Jake had been called several things he hadn't known were physically possible. All in all, though, shiny. The kids were so healthy in fact, that just two days after the procedure, they were ensconced in the cottage to stay. Both had dark hair, which didn't mean all that much at their age, but BMark had the pronounced O'Brian jaw line, and there was something around Mickie's eyes. There was no dark hair among the O'Brians, but Christy's was dark as night, so, no worries there, probably…

Of course Jen, just to be a pain, said Mikie looked like Grace, which made no sense at all. She said it with a wicked little smile, which made Ben laugh, and put a knot in Jake's stomach where one hadn't ever been before. His siblings were having a little too much fun with his new found angst.

And how did he feel about the babies? It was strange. He felt protective certainly. He felt an overwhelming obligation. He would certainly rip the throat out of anybody who tried to harm them. But did he love them? Did he? It was an intimidating thought. If he simply said yes and gave in, then there was love. An unbreakable bond of love. Oh, shit. A commitment. And then, what if, God forbid, something happened to them? Didn't other people just naturally love their children? As much as Ben and Jen bitched about the things their kids sometimes did, it was always clear that they always loved them. Maybe he wasn't "equipped," as Mark would put it, to love, even his own children. Maybe he was too much of a coward. Just like all the other times.

By mid December the cold weather had come. Jake had

Dale and Sam and their cohorts, Rex from the Hunter Fixall, and Rex's father, Mel, making regular deliveries of wood to the cottage, and still Christy and Jane, more Christy than Jane, complained of being cold. Kate, when she was over came wearing summer dresses.

"You're not going to drive me out, Uncle Jake," she'd joked. "It gets hot enough, I'll just strip down naked and pour some water on the hearth."

"No scandals, please," he'd said. He liked that kid. He could see she finally, grudgingly liked him. But if babies hadn't been on the way, he wondered if she would ever have come over. Was she coming out of familial obligation, or love? He knew she didn't really care for him a lot. He decided Kate did love him, but mostly out of familial obligation to do so. It confused him. He'd left the poor kid in the lurch. He'd left them all. Why were they taking such good care of him and Christy? Could it simply be that they were all good people? What a monumental shit he had been for most of his life! If there was a Mount Rushmore for shitheads, he'd be Washington. How could he not have known, for all this time, what great people were in his family? How could he not know how truly good they were?

Transcript—Session with Jake O'Brian.
Conducted by Mark O'Brian-Hicks, MS Psychology.

General Comments: Jake is having an awakening. Kind of like a kid about 23 years old. He's a late adolescent waking up.

Jake: Have they always been like this?
Myself: Who and like what?
Jake: Kate, Jen, Ben, well…you. All this stuff you're constantly doing for Christy and me and each other. Have you always been so… nice?
Myself: (Laughs) Jake, it's what you do for family.
Jake: I'm not sure you guys are different with anybody else.

Myself: No. No, you're probably right. It's what decent people do. They're…well…decent.

Jake: I'm not sure I have ever put myself out so much, just done something out of the goodness of my heart like that.

Myself:You remodeled the cottage for Christy and the babies.

Jake:Yeah, but why?

Myself: Okay, I'll bite.

Jake: I think I did it just to gratify myself. I did it just to control her.

Myself: I'm not sure you're as desperate a character as you think you are, Jake.You forget I knew you as a kid.You were always the nicest boy in the class to the girls. Even when the rest of us were calling them names, hitting them with books, because we didn't know what to do with our hormones.

Jake: (laughs) That's what players do, Mark.

Myself: Maybe, but there seemed like there was some goodness in there, too.

Jake:You see good because you are good.

Myself:Wow, who's the head shrinker here? Anyway, I'm not exactly a martyr. I've got the prettiest wife in town and I mooch off you and Ben all the time.

Jake: That's not mooching. That's coming to family gatherings, which you would do whether we were footing the bill or not.

Myself: Maybe.

Jake: Bullshit, "maybe." Mark, if I didn't have money, hadn't ever gone to college, I'd be rolling around in the muck with the drunks out at the River House, or in jail with those friends of Dale's. God that was a helluva thing.

Myself:Yeah, somebody should write a book.

Jake: How's she coming on that?

Myself: Almost done. It's off to the editors at the end of the week.

Jake: Any good?

Myself: Yeah. Yeah, it kinda opens out. Starts with a little commentary about how we've all lost our privacy, how everybody's life is fair game for the cameras and online media. How the truth gets distorted.We're all living a reality show… Pretty good writing. Ben was impressed too.

Jake: Well…if they need any legal help…

Myself: There you go again.

Jake: Huh?

Myself: Selfless as always.

Jake: Fuck off, Mark.

Myself: There's a good guy in there, Jake. I've always known it. And this from a guy that spent all of high school pissed at you.

Jake: Really?

Myself: Sure.

Jake: What for?

Myself: For being so damned good at everything. Three sport athlete, four if you count American Legion ball, star of the play, best voice in the school, star of the debate team, valedictorian, class president, and every girl within a 200 mile radius knew who you were and half of them slept with you by the time you were 16.

Jake: Yeah, that's what started me down the player trail. Honestly, though, most of that just happened. And once it started happening, I just kept letting it. And I started to cultivate it. I really liked it.

Myself: Well, who the hell wouldn't? You know, Jake, a lot of us are just good because it's what works best for us. A lot of us would have been afraid to put ourselves out there like you did, offer ourselves up for public consumption.

Jake: You make me sound like a barbecue at the Legion.

Myself: (laughs) Well, weren't you, kind of?

Jake: I never thought of it that way, but…

Myself: And there's a kind of selflessness in that. You became an object, an icon, mostly just by being you, through no real greed or lust, just because it came easy, and you went along.

Jake: I didn't have to.

Myself: No. But it would have taken a saint not to, wouldn't it?

Jake: (   ) Yeah. You know, you're right. And I'm no saint.

Myself: And neither are any of the rest of us. So, what you can do now is just keep doing what you're doing. Look out for Christy and the babies, however that turns out. Look out for the rest of us when trouble comes. And if trouble comes…

Jake: Yeah?

Myself: Stick around this time. Be there for Christy and the babies. Be there for us.

Jake: I think I can do that.

Myself: I think you can, too. There. You're all grown up. Want a Lifesaver?

Jake: (laughs) Fuck you, Hicks.

Myself: No really? Want one?

Jake: (laughs) Oh…yeah, sure.

December 19

Back at the cottage the stare down had begun. It was late morning by the time Jake arrived. In the previous week, Kate and Jen with Jane had decorated the cottage for Christmas. Special yuletide items from both families were everywhere. And Jake had just decorated the exterior with tasteful and expensive lights with a little help from Dale and Sam and Dale's boy, Donny, who even at, what, eleven, was already pretty handy and good for the high places… Jake had given them a sizable Christmas bonus. They had thanked him, wished him a Merry Christmas and good luck with the new family. He watched them get into Dale's old truck. Father and son and grandson. That was the way it was supposed to be. How could he make it that way for himself? It was likely he couldn't. First of all, his father was long dead. In truth, he'd barely known him, certainly not man-to-man the way Dale and Sam did. He'd only been Donny's age when the old man died. Second, he might not live until he had grandchildren, unless the twins had children before they were 30. That was far from a given these days among educated, white collar people like his family. Look at him. If he was going to be the model for his kids, and that was a scary thought, they might not start having kids, if at all, until they were in their 40s or even later like him. Even if he did have grandchildren, he wouldn't live to see them grow very old. Third, even to his children he would seem an old, old man. He'd be 67 when they were 10, 77 when they were 20. He'd be dead likely before they really arrived in the world where they were going to be. Does anybody ever really arrive where they're going to be? A high-powered career had all happened so fast for him, he had never really slowed down until the last few months. And now, needless to say, he hardly knew where he was.

Any way you looked at it, Christy was going to be doing most of the parenting. How did he feel about that? Could she really be trusted to take care of them? And what if she just took off again? What if he died unexpectedly, and left only Christy? Jane and Mick were great folks, and he liked the idea of the twins on that ranch, but they were too old. They'd already raised their kid, for better or worse. Christy was a beauty, but there was just no denying that she was a monumental piece of work. There was just no other way to look at it.

He needed another plan. He needed a fallback. Somebody needed to be there for those babies.

"Kate," he suddenly said aloud. It had just dropped into his head unbidden. Kate couldn't have children. She and David would make great parents. The twins would be blood relatives. Yes. He'd work up the papers. He'd make Kate and Dave legal guardians in the event of his death and/or Christy's…abandonment. Would Christy sign it? How would Jane and Mick feel about it? They were practical. And he'd seen Jane having several heart-to-hearts with Kate. I bet she'd like the idea. She knew how her daughter was. And, of course, Christy or no, he'd make sure the twins would visit in the West often, and Jane and Mick were always welcome here. He sighed.

"What a way to have to think."

He opened the back door, brushed off the snow in the tiny entry and opened the inner door, stepping up into the kitchen where good smelling things were in the offing.

Kate was baking cookies.

"Hi, kiddo."

"I hate…"

"I know, you hate to be called that." He leaned over her and kissed the top of her head.

"To what do I owe this great honor?"

"Just for being you."

Despite herself, and not without a quizzical look, Kate smiled. Then she looked back down at her work. "Thanks."

Jake proceeded into the living room.

"Everything shiny here?"

Jane looked up from her embroidery. "We're fine, Jake. Just fine. Could you put some more wood…"

"Already on it." He stoked the fire, and walked over to kiss Christy, who turned her cheek so he pecked her there. He looked into the bassinet where the kids were asleep and entangled with each other, just as they'd been in the womb no doubt.

"How's Mommy?"

"Don't call me that."

"Okay."

There was palpable tension in the room. Jake nearly continued out the front door and down to the lake, but he made himself stay. Finally, Jane spoke.

"Christy has something to tell you, Jake. You want me to leave the room, dear?"

"No. No. You can hear. You've heard it already."

This was going to be it. Her could tell. He wasn't the babies' father. He didn't know if he wanted to hear that, but he was going to anyway. He could see it in Christy's dark eyes. He tried to prepare himself. He didn't know how to prepare himself.

"The babies are Bump's children." She said it as coldly as if she were announcing a plane schedule.

"W-what?"

"You heard me," she turned her pretty face to the window facing the lake.

Of course. Of course they were. Why hadn't it ever occurred…

"You're sure."

"Positive."

"How can you be so…"

"Because the pregnancy lines up almost to the day. It was the week before the wedding, that office party when you were in

Paris and we were back in Washington, finishing up the Georgian constitution changes…"

"Oh, yeah. You worked on that a long time," he said absently.

Wow. Wow.

Her voice was still expressionless when she added, "We work well together. We were drunk. It just happened."

He felt like a church bell without a clapper. There was nothing to say. He wasn't surprised and yet he was. Why hadn't he suspected….? He'd never have thought the kid had it in him. Fucking your boss's wife, well, that took…balls. Inadvertently he laughed aloud, then caught himself.

Both Christy and Jane shot him a look. When he stopped and looked at Christy, she looked back towards the window. Jane kept her eyes on him and her look was, concern. Concern for *his* welfare. Wherever Christy got her devious streak, it wasn't from Jane.

He almost laughed again, but stopped himself. It was funny, not just for the obvious pun, but because he couldn't believe his feeling of detachment. Was this feeling his new emotional and spiritual evolution, or was this him slipping back into good ol' Shiny? He didn't feel even an ounce of anger. He didn't feel anything but a kind of relief that he knew now. She wasn't lying. Jane would never have let her say something she thought was a lie. And she always knew her daughter's lies. She knew her daughter. Then something else dropped down into his mind. At first, it seemed unrelated, but then he saw a logical connection. Maybe… Maybe Bump was ready to take over the business. What an odd thought. And yet it seemed dead on to him. Christy had apparently helped Bump develop himself into just the kind of scoundrel one needed to be to work in the world of high-powered, international law. And he'd better not give Christy all the credit, or blame. Jake had been the primary model for Bump. And, oh God, maybe for Christy, too. Had he ruined…had Shiny ruined two decent young people with his example? Like almost everything else in that other life he'd led, he'd never given the welfare of those two young people, who were using him as an example, any thought at all. Or was that all delusions of grandeur. Maybe *everything* that he'd done until now, everything, didn't amount to anything at all. Maybe he'd lived a life without influence, aimlessly piling up money, among the superficial people, the egomaniacs who ran the world. Maybe Christy and Bump had been shits just like old Shiny, just like Jake, long before he'd met either of them.

"Jesus…"

He could feel Jane's eyes on him. Christy was still looking out the window. All this, all his selfish worry about his impact or lack of impact in the world was beside the point. It was past. He couldn't do one useful thing about that now. He looked into the basinet. The babies still slept. They would be awake soon, all too soon. And they'd need care. Somebody had to take care of them. He was going to be that somebody. He felt tears welling into his eyes. And another thought came to him. He did love them, certainly as much as he loved anybody in his family, and probably much more, or at least differently. And what he was about to do had to do with that and that alone. His next move locked down into place, rock solid. Solid as life-long love. He'd work up the papers making Kate and David legal guardians in the event of his death or Christy's, and in the event of Christy's abandonment of the babies. That last would be a hard sell, but he was a hard-nosed lawyer. He was sure Jane would see the logic in it, and he'd make her his ally. She already was his ally. Then, he'd work up papers turning the law firm over to Bump. All of it. Then he'd set up a trust fund for the babies, a salary for consulting for himself and Christy, the whole golden parachute routine. All dependent upon Bump making no claim on the babies. It was a win-win. If Bump wanted some part in the raising of the children, then he was a better person than Jake had been up to this point and the kids would be fine anyway. If he didn't, then things were just as he estimated, and this plan would suit perfectly. He'd start on it all today. First he'd talk to Kate and David. He felt absolutely certain of their answer.

Then a small explosion went off in his newly opened heart. *Oh, but what if Christy intended to leave him for Bump?*

"You know…"

Christy turned to him. Jane looked up from her embroidery.

"It doesn't matter."

"You're…not mad?"

"Might have been, even a couple weeks ago. Might have been, but not now. It's shiny."

"Really?"

"Yup. I'm going to work up the papers…" he said absently, almost inadvertently.

"Do you think a divorce is a good idea, Jake? Best for the babies?" Jane was speaking levelly. She'd given this a lot of thought.

"Divorce? No, no. I mean, I'm going to turn the firm over to Bump. That'll keep him busy. The babies, well, they're ours, Christy. And there's an end." He met her eyes, for just a moment becoming the calculating cold-hearted lawyer again.

"Really?" Her voice was still strangely emotionless. "No divorce?"

"No divorce." Her expression changed, and he just caught a glimpse of it as Christy turned back to the lake. Was it his imagination, or did she look disappointed?

January 9

By early January, the true snow had come, though not the cold. Jake was relieved of that at least. Still, Jane, who he could tell was getting homesick, and Christy were cold every day. Jane only suggested he put more wood on the fire, often. There was no shortage of it and he was glad to do it. Christy, was another story. She was angry. Just angry. The doctor wouldn't commit on whether it was postpartum depression. At any rate, to say she was not taking new motherhood gracefully was well…understatement. Kate still moved silently about the house, endearing herself, without really trying to. Kate and David had readily and gratefully agreed to guardianship in case of his and Christy's demise. However, Kate had been very reluctant about the abandonment clause, "Jake, they're Christy's kids! We can't agree to that. Unless…unless you think she might endanger…"

Kate had looked Jake directly in the eyes, and he had begun to weep. Kate's eyes had opened wide in surprise, "Oh…my god… Uncle Jake. I…I didn't know. I'm so, so sorry."

"I don't understand," David had said, looking quizzically at both of them.

"Christy…is…just like me," Jake said.

Kate took Jake's hand and looked at him with Grace's eyes. It startled him. "Just like you used to be," she said.

Christy, had signed the papers, too, with only a moment or two of crying over the idea, and then a question about the "abandonment" clause.

"It's just a formality. I've included myself under that clause too, you'll notice. Look, we've both left this marriage before. We've got to protect the kids."

"Bullshit," Christy had said and began to weep. "You think I'm an unfit mother."

But the tears had subsided, quite quickly. She'd signed and stormed out of the room, slamming the door.

As for Bump, it was news to him that the children were his. His immediate reaction, when he and Jake met in Jake's Washington law office, was fairly predictable. "Christy is probably lying."

"It could be."

"I'm not going to get saddled with it, Jake, unless there's a paternity test. Don't…don't you want to raise them as your own?"

There was not an ounce of concern for the children in his voice.

Jake, or was it Shiny, sprang the trap, "There might be another option for you. A pretty good one."

Bump had signed the papers before Jake even finished explaining. Jake was ashamed if he had created this monster, but for the babies' sakes, he was almost glad he had.

In the coming weeks, something very interesting and disconcerting started to happen with Christy. She became very deferential towards Kate, seeking out her advice, confiding "secrets" to her. Kate was taking it all with a grain of salt, the way Grace would have. There was not an ounce of evil in that girl. What she wanted most, Jake could see, was for Christy to be a good mother. All she asked in return was the opportunity to be a good aunt. She was good. Truly good. Jake could never really aspire to that level of goodness, but at least his niece could be a model for him of what a good person is like.

Too late for me, but maybe I can teach the babies to be like her.

Jane watched her daughter closely, sadly, Jake thought. There was hope in those looks, but not much. Christy's father, Mick, called now and then. Something he had never done before. He needed his wife, though he wasn't saying it. Just made jokes for everybody.

"Old cowboys don't do well alone," Jane said bemused. "I miss that man."

"Well," Jake said, "we'll get you back there soon. Soon as you want really. Then we'll come out and visit with the babies."

"Whatever," Christy said. Both Jane and Jake ignored her.

Jen, now finished with the book and consulting with the editors, was living and working at the O'Brian camp next door while Ben was out in Iowa visiting Val. Mark came out after work at the prison each evening. Ben had insisted that she spend the nights to take care of Huck and Tom. She was spoiling both rotten, as Ben had known she would. Her work next door also offered her an opportunity to flit in and out of the lake house, getting the scoop. One day, while Jake was visiting at camp, Jake told Jen the truth about the babies. Jen's eyes got big. Jake had decided there was no point in hiding it. She was going to find out. He'd told her about all the legal papers too and all the conversations and everybody's reactions. He'd made her promise not to spill to anyone else, only Mark, who was as safe with secrets as the CIA.

She'd bitten her lip. But he'd seen the look of determination come into her eyes. "Okay. Okay. Nobody but Mark and Huck and Tom."

"They're all good with secrets," Jake had said, managing a smile.

"But how are you with this?"

"Let's just get the babies on their feet. Let's just get everybody safely through into tomorrow."

Jen's eyes got wide again, and there were tears standing in them. "Jake…"

He looked at her and couldn't read her full expression. "What?"

"You're…you're growing up."

"You think?"

"Yes. I wasn't sure I'd ever see it happen."

"Truth?"

She nodded.

"I wasn't either."

She smiled at him. Then began to cry full out and hugged him. He looked out the camp's porch window across the lake and then glanced at the woods, beyond which was the cottage next door. He and Jen had worn a sizable path there going back and forth. He didn't even need to shovel.

"Yup," he said, when the hug was through. "Shiny."

In late January, in the heart of winter, one morning two weeks after Ben and Val had returned from their holiday time in Iowa, Ben's old friend, the old labrador, Huck, Ben's rock through the troubles and change of the last 14 years, just didn't wake up.

"Only Huck could go that way," the vet and long-time friend of Ben's, Jeff Jesson said, after tearfully examining the old dog. He had insisted upon rushing over, against Ben's protests that it was already too late, just to see his old hunting buddy one last time, Ben surmised. He would always be grateful to Jeff for that. And, God knew, the old dog had come back before, why not this time?

"No trouble for anybody," Ben said to Jeff, when the vet confirmed Ben's first suspicions. "Just did his job to the last."

"I guess he figured you'll be all right now, Ben," Jeff said.

Ben, who would cry himself out on a ski across to the narrow open channel at the far end of Hunter Lake with Tom and Val later that morning, said to Jeff, "I guess I will be."

"You guess?" Val said, throwing her arms around him right

there in front of Jeff.

"I know."

Tom, the young lab, stood nearby wagging his tail slowly. Jeff reached down a hand and patted him.

"You're in charge of these folks now, Tom. Can you handle them?"

Ben, straining a bit, said, "He'll be just fine."

On January 30, with the snow three feet deep around the camp and cottage and Dale and John and Donnie coming out daily to plow and shovel, though Ben insisted on scooping out his paths on his own, Jen found a letter at the camp while Ben was out on a long ski with Tom.

The letter was mostly open on the porch dining table. She only edged it out of the envelope a bit. It read in part:

"I think your idea is great! You're such a crusty old romantic. A wedding at the

train station in Harbinger. Just the two of us on the day we met. Spring in the Winter of our lives. Or late Fall at least. Do you think we can keep it a secret, from my sisters? From Jen? Ha! I love you, Ben.

Val."

How in the world was she going to keep this secret?

February 3

"Bless me, Father, for I have sinned…"

"Something wrong, my son?"

"Bill, is it okay if I just bring this chair around and sit so I can face you?"

"Sure."

Jake moved the "confession chair" which had been backed up against Father Bill's in the space at the base of the bell tower, around so he was facing Father Bill, who, to accommodate, backed his chair off a foot or so.

"Hello, Jake," Father Bill said sardonically, having known full well whom he was talking to anyway, and also aware that Jen had demanded Jake go to confession before the babies were baptized.

The two had known each other for only a few years as a result of Jen having dragged Jake to Mass a time or two.

"How long's it been?"

"It has been 40 years since my last…"

Father Bill laughed and ran his hand over his bald head and strands of thinning gray hair. "No, I mean since we've seen each other."

"Oh…ha…old choir boys die hard. I guess a couple years."

"Big doings since, to hear Jen tell it."

"Oh, she tells it all right. Just life really."

"Everything good?"

"Shiny."

"Ha, Ben warned me about that."

"What?"

"'Shiny'. He says it's what you say when you're blowing people off."

"I guess he's right… Should we talk about my sins?"

"If you like."

"Well, that's one of them: blowing people off. Maybe my biggest one. Sins of omission, not doing what I should have done, starting all the way back with my dad's death, but also with Ben's wife Grace's and Mom's. I've never been there for people, and I want to learn how to be there for the babies."

"I like a man who gives a priest specific direction."

"Sorry."

"No, I mean that."

"Oh, good."

"Okay. I think this is fairly easy to look at logically. It's a simple matter of presence, Jake. Then, once you're there, it becomes a matter of reacting to what's in front of you. Not having raised kids, I don't know for sure, but I have helped out with a lot of family situations, and I'm guessing that reacting well to all the crazy stuff they're likely to do or encounter will be the key from now on."

"Huh, you're pretty good at this."

"I've had practice."

"So do you want me to enumerate?"

"Enumerate?"

"How many times I did this or that or didn't do this or that…"

"If you want, but neglecting your children even once is too many and doing so a million, million times will be forgiven anyway, so what's the point of counting?"

"Jeez, what kind of priest are you?" Jake smiled broadly.

"A tired one."

Father Bill made the sign of the cross over Jake. "Go and sin no more."

"I don't think…"

"It's wishful thinking, Jake. Hoping against hope. Having faith. Don't take it literally. Nobody ever really goes and sins no more."

In the little church by the lake, later that afternoon, the baptisms took place, attended by only a few and heated by a space heater in the corner of the altar as the lake church wasn't usually open this far into winter. Jen had insisted that this was the place to do it. Jane had been quite satisfied, since the little church made her nostalgic for a similar chapel on the family ranch. Father Bill made a habit of never crossing strong women, especially from the O'Brian family. Jake was unsurprised by his sister's insistence, quite pleased that she was handling things. Religion was an area in which he felt completely incompetent. Ben, who was acting as godfather, to Jen's godmother to the babies, was typically bemused.

Father Bill was intrigued by Ben's attendance at church, a presence that would be repeated often in the coming weeks down at the church on campus in Hunter. Asking around, Father Bill had found out from Ben's friend, devout Catholic, and former colleague at Hunter Woods College's English department, Matt

"Mutt" Esposito, that Ben hadn't been to Mass in ages.

"He's changed since he met Val," Mutt had told the priest. "Definitely for the better."

Christy was indifferent and barely smiled throughout the ceremony.

Later that afternoon, when Jake dropped off Jane at the airport in Pellston, on the first leg of her long trip back to Reno, his mother-in-law, only six years his senior, was candid. "If I'm reading Christy right…"

"I'm sure you are."

She nodded grimly. "If I'm reading her right, you've got trouble coming. It's not postpartum, if you're wondering. It's just Christy. She's brooding about something."

"Do you mind telling me what?"

Jane bit her lip for a moment and readjusted one of her bags on her shoulder. Jake was carrying two others. "I'm only guessing, Jake, but I think the father might be involved."

"Bump?" It surprised him, and when he thought about it later, he wondered why. Of course she was thinking of Bump, if Bump was really the father.

Jane was nodding pensively again. "Yes."

Jake had to ask, "Are you sure…?"

Jane shook her head, "No, I'm not at all certain she's telling the truth about that. I was, but I'm not. I'm not certain what she's up to Jake. The babies could be yours, but…" she was starting to well up.

Jake patiently helped her along after a moment, "But…"

"Oh dear, I don't want to hurt you, Jake…"

"Go ahead."

"All right. Jake, I'm not really sure she wants them to be yours… If they are."

Jake was suddenly at a total loss. Though he wasn't sure why it surprised him so much. He'd known that this might well be true: that Christy didn't love him, maybe never had. But the heart comes to such knowledge long after the head.

"I'm sorry."

"Sh-shiny. It's not your fault."

Watching the plane depart, he was tempted to wait around another few hours for the next outbound flight, anywhere. But that would mean leaving Christy, and, more importantly, leaving the babies. If he did that, he would never forgive himself, and he could never go back. And then, he'd be his old self again: his old shiny self. And, he suddenly realized, and this was a very pleasant surprise, that he never wanted to be that guy again.

March 21

As calendar Spring approached and with it the anniversary of Ben and Val's rendezvous on the train, which was also the date for the planned wedding, Jen was on high alert regarding her oldest brother, but not regarding either of those cheerful concerns. She was worried about the fact that Ben had yet to scatter Huck's ashes, and that the anniversary of the old dog's recovery from a massive stroke was also coming soon. Ben had tipped off Val when she arrived at the camp that Jen was hanging around, asking him questions about how he was feeling. Val at first wrote it off as Jen's busybody nature, but soon saw signs that Ben was not so cheerful as he had been in most of the time she'd known him.

"What do I do?" she asked Jen on a visit to her future sister-in-law's house in Hunter.

"If he mentions anything about going on an extended ski and starts packing things in his backpack, let me know."

"He only skis down to the channel and back. He doesn't need anything other than the water in the... What would he pack?"

"Huck's ashes."

"Oh..."

"My brother is in love with you, Val." She was having a dreadful time at that moment not spilling the beans and telling Val she knew about the wedding. Of course, she'd told a few people. She, well, she just thought it wasn't right for that secret to be completely kept. "... and I've never seen him happier, but what goes up must come down. A person's basic nature doesn't completely change, at least not Ben's, not forever. I believe you've made him a much better, more stable person but..."

"Thank you, Jen. That's very sweet." Val said. For a second she thought about the suspicious, angry woman she'd first met at the door of this house about a year ago, and smiled. That relationship had certainly changed.

"But my brother loves those he loves fiercely, and when they die, it affects him deeply. Because of you, Huck's death has only tainted the edges for him, but remembering the train, followed so close by Huck's miracle come back, is going to take him way up, and what goes up... Anyway, if you see him packing a backpack and seeming a little, well, distracted. Let me know. He shouldn't be alone."

Sure enough, Ben was all joy on the anniversary of the train meeting and their wedding. They'd said to everyone in Hunter that they were going on the train from Lansing and taking it to Harbinger for a visit, to commemorate the the anniversary of their meeting. All true.

As they pulled into the Harbinger, Iowa train station, Ben and Val were standing on the steps down to the tracks with their bags over their shoulders. To both of their amazements, there was a crowd waiting. And in it were a lot of tall thin, attractive women, and a few hefty farm girls, clearly Val's close relatives. Ben looked at Val suspiciously, but she shook her head, smiled and shrugged. Near them were a mess of rowdy kids, tugging at their ties and dresses, some hard handed old farmers, and a thin blonde woman who looked...

"Jesus," Ben said. "That's, Jen!"

And near her a dark young woman who looked remarkably like...Grace.

"Kate!"

Waiting at the train stop in Harbinger, along with the Traeger family and the justice of the peace, were also Mark, David, Jake without Christy, Michael, Collin, even Sean, Mutt, Ray Antilla, and Jeff Jesson along with a host of the rest of Val's family and friends.

"I don't know why I'm so surprised. At some level, I knew this would happen." Ben said.

"I did too. Val said. "You mad at your sister?"

Ben smiled. It was truly hilarious that both he and Val had quickly reached the same conclusion.

"Nah, but she doesn't need to know that."

Val stifled a laugh as they greeted their unexpected guests at the train stop.

The newlyweds were joyous at the surprise reception at the Legion Hall across the street, catered by Val's sister Bunny's restaurant.

Sure enough, though, as Jen had also predicted, one day about two weeks later, back at the camp, when another March blizzard hit, then subsided, Ben was packing a backpack.

"I'm going on a little bit longer run today, sweety," he said to Val, who hadn't forgotten.

"Want some company?"

"Um…sure."

Val texted Jen and made a point of delaying things a bit by changing her clothes several times. By the time the two of them arrived at the channel, Mark, Jen, Jake, even Kate, who called in at the school with a family emergency were there, having driven to within a quarter mile of the channel via a logging road off to the east of the lake and snowshoeing the remaining distance.

Ben was smiling, and only slightly tearful, when he said, to Huck's memory, "Well bud, I thought we'd have a private moment, but as usual…"

"Doofus," Jen said.

"Sneak."

Ben scattered the ashes while singing "Star of the County Down." Everyone sang along.

It was a good day, with many more good days coming.

"All will be well…" Ben said into the night, later that evening, listening to Val's endearing little snore as they lay in bed. And he truly believed it.

May 15

Speaking of happiness, when May came, Christy was the picture of it. She had suddenly taken to motherhood and to Hunter Lake, and Jake began to believe that it had been postpartum after all.

The chilly air, which kept off the bugs, made it possible to go on all kinds of hikes around the lake. Christy was game, and each of them carried a baby in a front pack wherever they went.

Had she really come to grips with herself? Jake wondered.

Then one morning, after announcing that she was going for groceries and taking the babies along and that Jake didn't need to bother, Christy and the babies disappeared.

Jake was frantic. He called Jane immediately. Jane said she had just that moment gotten off the phone with Christy.

"I was just about to call you."

Jake absolutely believed her.

"She seemed very calm," Jane said. "The babies are fine, but she says she's left you, and she's going to be filing for divorce."

"I…"

The tears were suddenly flowing out of Jake, but he managed to ask, "Did she mention Bump?"

"Yes, Jake. She says they're going to be married. I think they've been planning it for months."

"Shiny," Jake said, and stifled some more tears.

"You better do what you need to do."

Jake was suddenly calm. What came next would involve the law. He knew the law. And he knew the law was cold, but he would do what he could, using the papers which had already been signed and using every neuron in his fertile legal mind to make things turn out the way he intended.

"She's not taking those kids away from me, Jane."

"Nor should she."

By midday, Jake had made the calls and filed most of the divorce and proposed joint custody papers. Christy and Bump were served at the airport in Washington, the moment she got off the plane. The legal fight had begun, and Jake was going to win all he could. He had no intention of being cruel, but he was going to get a favorable result.

By noon the next day, the revamped papers signing over the legal firm to Bump and Christy, with a golden parachute for Jake in place, were in Bump's hands. Bump actually called.

"Jake…I…don't know what to say. This is unbelievable."

"Say you'll take the deal, right now, or it's gone forever."

"Oh…okay."

"And as the deal stipulates, there is to be no genetic testing of the children or legal wrangling concerning my joint custody with Christy. You are not in the picture, except as one of their day-to-day guardians."

"I don't know if Christy…"

"I'll deal with Christy."

An hour later his phone rang and it was Christy. "Jake, be reasonable. The babies aren't yours. Bump is their biological father and he has a right to be seen as such."

"In every real sense, except maybe one, those children most certainly are mine, as well as yours, and perhaps Bump's."

"You doubt Bump's the father?"

"Darlin', I doubt everything you say."

There was a long pause and then very audible sobbing for a suspiciously short interval.

"I'll have to talk to my parents."

"Go ahead. Jane is on board with me."

"I'll talk to Daddy then."

"Go ahead. What are you going to tell him? I'm not cutting you out. I'm not even really cutting Bump out. In fact I'm giving both of you a helluva a deal. I just don't want to be cut out of my children's lives…"

"They're not…"

"Christy, you better think long and hard about what you're going to say next. You know how well I know the law. I can have those kids genetically tested. If that test shows that Bump isn't the father, there will be more legal papers coming your way. Some of them will have to do with something called 'mental cruelty' regarding our divorce and custody arrangement, and some others will have to do with the law firm itself and your and Bumps' rights to it. What I have offered you so far, I am only offering you out of love. I still love you, and I'll take you back any time, but darlin', you're not going to screw me in the courts. You're in my backyard, kiddo, and Bump is a baby. If I wanted, I could tear him to pieces."

There was a long pause on the other end of the line, minus the sobs this time. "So, summers on Hunter Lake for the babies."

"And Christmas and Thanksgiving. Until they reach the age of consent. You and Bump can even be here if you like. If you look close, I've bought up an extra lot to build a second house."

"Okay. But this bullshit about 'in case of abandonment' you get full custody has got to go. I didn't like it when I first signed it. I didn't like the implications. I'm not that person, Jake, whatever you may think. I'm not going to abandon my children."

"Again, it's just a formality. I've included myself under the clause too, given my track record, like I told you before."

"Bullshit, I won't sign it then…"

Jake was tired of mincing words. "Yes, you will darlin'… I'm tired of all this posturing. You've got thirty seconds to agree to sign and two hours to fax me a copy of the signed documents."

The pause on the other end of the line lasted less than five seconds. "And it's still Kate and David as guardians in the unlikely event that both of us die or…"

"Yup."

"Well, I do like that."

"So do I."

Three seconds of silence and one, audible sigh ensued. Then…

"Okay. It's a deal."

June 1

The divorce was final in record time. Bump and Christy were off on their honeymoon, and the babies were back at Hunter Lake by the time the mosquitos got bad. The bugs didn't matter much. The cabin was air tight, and Jake was, for the most part, inside with the babies, aided daily by Kate and Jen, who was amazed at Jake's new maternal nature.

"People change, sis."

"Not this much. Not forever."

They sat in the living room watching Mickie and B.Mark exploring their new world. They were delightfully unfussy babies. Jen said she wondered if Jake could have handled anything else. They slept through the night and hardly seemed to miss their mother.

"I wonder how much time she actually spent with them." Jen said.

"I wonder that too."

July 1

On July first, the letter arrived. It was on personal stationery and seemed tear-stained. He wondered about the tears, but decided to give Christy the benefit of the doubt. He'd been just like her once:

Dear Jake,

I only know one way to say this: I'm an unfit mother. Bump, is in love with the business. He's left me. I don't even seem to care. I'm going on a trip around the world with the money you left me, and I'm suing Bump for two-thirds of the business. I'll get back to you when I return from my trip. If I return.

In some ways I still love you, especially for how decent you've been about all of this. My mom is ashamed of me. My dad is too, I think, but won't say it.

When the babies can understand, try to speak kindly of me, though I wouldn't blame you if you didn't. Still, I'm no different now from what I was when you married me. Really, I'm no different from the way you used to be. You're the one who's changed, not me. I thought I could be a wife and mother, maybe because that's what my folks wanted, but it was never in the cards.

I think the best favor I will ever do Mickie and little Ben, is to stay out of their lives.

I think the best favor I can do for you is to never see you again. Then again, you never know.

Love,

Christy.

August 3

In early August, Ben's friend, Mutt, died, leaving a vacancy in the English department at Hunter Woods College. Kate applied, and with her local connections, razor-sharp mind, and incredible credentials, she was quickly hired. All she lacked was a PhD, and as a condition of her employment, started on her doctorate immediately, somehow never neglecting, in the years to come, her new nephew and niece.

She was the closest thing to a mother they would ever have.

September 15

In the Fall, the babies, now nearly a year old, were delighting the family with their antics. Jane, who visited often, told everyone tales of the babies' Western ancestors. Mick just smiled and nodded, watching them when Jake brought the babies out to the ranch, which was often, in the years to come.

Mickie was a climber; B.Mark was curious about books. Go figure. There was absolutely no word from Christy, according to Jane, who seemed resigned and saddened, by her daughter's behavior regarding her own children. She had warned Jake not to mention their Christy to Mick.

"Old cowboys don't cry often," she said. "but they cry hard."

October 14

To clear up any possible future legal hassles Jake finally did have the babies genetically tested. He was curious, but not overly so. His razor-sharp legal mind, seeing all possible future outcomes, could see no reason not to hedge his bets. Life is long, he knew, and full of courtrooms when it came to dealing with once-warring parties, even in times of peace. He sent off the genetic materials he'd gathered from the babies on a crisp but lovely Fall day on which he made Ben happy by begging off hunting. Instead, he spent a morning going through some old business in his new home office.

Within a week, he had all but forgotten about sending out the test materials, and about the possible outcomes resulting from the report which he would get back in a few weeks. Life on Hunter Lake simply went on, as usual.

Thanksgiving

The test results were in. They'd come a week before and were in an envelope with a lot of other mail he hadn't looked at yet. The whole family, literally everyone, Ben and Val, Jen and Mark, Michael, Sean, Collin, Kate and David, even the Sylvanus family with all their new relations, were present at the newly expanded Jake O'Brian cottage. Ike's wife, Dale's daughter-in-law, Donya, was sitting near and conversing with her new colleague, Kate. She was gracious towards Jake, but he did catch a bemused smile each time she looked his way. She was still on guard. Probably always would be. Good for her.

The expansion of the cottage had been accomplished by, of course, the Sylvanuses and included two new bedrooms and bathrooms for the twins, creating a new west wing, and the legal office for Jake off the east wing. The "cottage" had become more of a minor estate. What Jake termed a "lake house." Ben had predictably rolled his eyes at the phrase, as Jake had known he would, which was the main reason he had used it. Jake intended to use the office to deal with the legal troubles of friends and family only, but business had begun to expand, with Jake's expanding list of old and new Hunter friends. There were even a few clients from Newberry.

"Don't let this get out of hand," Jen had sternly warned him. "Those babies need you."

As the festivities continued, on that chilly Thanksgiving, with just a dusting of snow outside, Jake took a moment to sort through his mail and found the test results. He left the business papers and a couple of friendly letters and invitations on the front hall table to be taken to the office later. Then he walked, with the results in his right hand and the junk mail in his left, towards the roaring hearth. He pulled back the screen and tossed the junk mail in. Shutting the screen, he turned to go into the kitchen to see how preparations for dinner were coming. Jen had banished everyone else from her work space, telling them to enjoy the day. Once he himself was inevitably banished again, he planned to go into his office and take just a moment with the test results. What stopped him was seeing Ben and Val with Kate, all those now grown nephews, and, of course, the babies. The nephews were telling edgy hip jokes, and Ben was laughing with Mickie as she investigated his nose and tried to crawl over his shoulder. Val looked on, delighted. Kate, was reading *Where the Wild Things Are* to wide-eyed and completely attentive B.Mark. Jake looked down at the envelope containing the test results, then back up at his family. He hesitated only a moment.

He reopened the screen and tossed the envelope into the fire.

"Shiny," he whispered, as it was slowly consumed.

Acknowledgements

Thank you to Editor-in-Chief, Matt Dryer, and Book Editors U.P. Poet Laureate Marty Achatz and Monica Nordeen; my performance partner in *Under This Cold Sky*, Steve Hooper with whom I've shared big crowds, small crowds, and no crowds in promoting the Hunter Lake line; the folks at Snowbound Books, The Marquette Regional History Center, Uptown Gifts, Snyder's, Falling Rock Cafe and Books, U.P. Trading Company, Peter White Public Library, The Marquette Mining Journal, TV6 and TV10 Marquette, and all other media outlets who helped with publicity; Tom Powers and the folks of Michigan in Books; Shelley Russell and Beverly Matherne, of Northern Michigan University, and Helen Haskell Remien of The Joy Center; those who have followed the book announcements and publicity on tumblr at *bgbradleyauthor.tumblr.com* and all those who have followed the poetry, book excerpts and random thoughts for the last few years on the Facebook page: "North Words with Beeg;" and last, but certainly not least, my colleagues, students, fans, friends, and my loving family. This book exists because of each and every one of you. On we go! Meet you at Ray's Sugar Shack for the next one and after that…well…you'll see.

ABOUT THE AUTHOR

B.G. BRADLEY is a retired high school teacher, former newspaper reporter and columnist, part time college professor, poet, novelist, playwright, director and actor. His fiction, non-fiction, and poetry have appeared in various regional publications including *Detroit Sunday Magazine*, *Michigan Out-of-Doors*, *Passages North*, *Sidewalks*, *Foxcry Review*, *The Marquette Mining Journal*, and *The Newberry News*. His plays have appeared on local stages including the Lake Superior Theatre which in 2010 produced his *Lake Stories*, the Hunter Lake books, which he wrote, directed, and starred in as Ben O'Brian opposite NMU's Dr. Shelley Russell as Grace. Bradley lives in Diorite with the love of his life, Debbie, and his labradors, Tom and Sam. His sons Taggart and Patrick are actors and arts activists on their own.

Coming soon from Benegamah Press...

At the
SUGAR SHACK

I'm making you a reservation for Camp
Grossy. You know, Ray Antilla's place, the rambling
sugar shack above the Gros Rocher River near
Hunter. Everybody, I mean everybody is going to
be there. It will be maple syrup season. All the trees
will be tapped, the sap will be boiling. The wind
will be in the maples and slipping in through the
many cracks in Camp Grossy, but you'll be warm.
Every one of your friends will be there. Ben, Jen,
Jake, Katie, Michael, Dale and Carrie, lots of others
you know, and many other natives of Hunter
you've not yet met, but who will seem immediately
familiar and inevitable. What's more, every one of
them is going to tell you their story, as the sap boils
and the night wears on.
See you soon *At the Sugar Shack.*

Made in the USA
Lexington, KY
09 November 2019

56746313R00070